Mojo Rising

Also by James L. Dickerson

Devil's Sanctuary
An Eyewitness History of Mississippi Hate Crimes
with Alex A. Alston

Inside America's Concentration Camps
Two centuries of Internment and Torture

Yellow Fever
A Deadly Disease Poised To Kill Again

The Hero Among Us
Memoirs of an FBI Witness Hunter
with Jim Ingram

Mojo Triangle
Birthplace of Country, Blues, Jazz and Rock 'n' Roll

Just for a Thrill
Lil Hardin Armstrong, First Lady of Jazz

Dixie's Dirty Secret
How the Government, the Media, and the Mob
Reshaped the Modern Republican Party
Into the Image of the Old Confederacy

Scotty & Elvis
Aboard the Mystery Train
with Scotty Moore

Memphis Going Down
A Century of Blues, Soul, and Rock 'n' Roll

Mojo Rising

Masters of the Art
A Short Story Anthology

Edited by
James L. Dickerson

Mojo Triangle™ Books
an imprint of

SARTORIS
LITERARY
GROUP

A traditional publisher with a non-traditional approach to publishing

To Mardi Allen, who encouraged me to pursue
the dream of putting this book together
and
The late Dr. John Pilkington, Professor of English,
my American literature mentor at
the University of Mississippi

CONTENTS

Mojo Rising

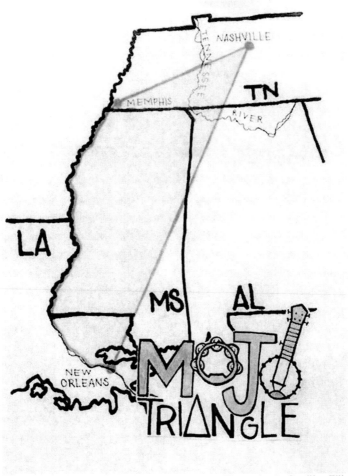

Illustration by Sterlling Ellis

What is the Mojo Triangle?

Draw a straight line from New Orleans to Nashville, then over to Memphis and back down to New Orleans following the curves of the Mississippi River, and you have the Mojo Triangle, a geometrical, cultural, and spiritual configuration that represents the geographical birthplace of America's original music—Country, Blues, Jazz, and Rock 'n' Roll—and the home of America's most powerful and innovative literature.

INTRODUCTION

The idea for this book began when I was a 17-year-old freshman at the University of Mississippi, though I didn't realize at the time that I was even remotely capable of hatching a literary concept. William Faulkner, my literary hero, had died the previous year. For some reason I don't recall, I felt it was acceptable for his sister-in-law, Dorothy Oldham, to give me a private tour of the Faulkner home, Rowan Oak. I found a listing for her in the telephone book, gave her a call, and, to my surprise, she agreed to meet me at the home for an exclusive tour.

I was embarrassed that my head had been shaved, the initiation at the time for freshman men, but she hardly seemed to notice and was most gracious, at one point leaving me alone in Mr. Faulkner's office while she checked on the upstairs plumbing. At the time I did not know that such tours were a rarity, making me one of the few people to see the home the way Mr. Faulkner had left it when he walked out the door to go to the hospital, never to return.

That visit to Rowan Oak inspired me to delve deeper into American literature. As a freshman I had read half of the books penned by Mr. Faulkner; by the time I was graduated from the university with a major in English and psychology, I had copies of everything he had ever written in my library. I was lucky to find an English professor, Dr. John Pilkington, who was willing to mentor me in my exploration of Southern literature. While that was going on, I helped pay my way through college by playing in rock and blues bands, all of which were campus based. It amazed me that so much of America's music had originated in a geographical area I subsequently named the Mojo Triangle—blues, rock and roll, jazz and country music. Over the years, I realized the same thing had happened with American literature. The most innovative literature in America had also originated within the geographical boundaries of the Mojo Triangle. The writers from that geographical area had more in common with each other than they did with writers elsewhere in the country.

This book offers an acknowledgment of the literary fires that have burned brightly within the Mojo Triangle. We have a second volume, *Mojo Rising: Contemporary Writers*, edited by University of Mississippi journalism professor Joseph B. Atkins, that focuses on Mojo writers who honed their writing skills in the years following Mr. Faulkner's death in 1962 and continue to carry the torch.

My interest in Mr. Faulkner continued after I left the university and went on to forge a career as a journalist. Along the way I befriended one of the writer's early friends Ben Wasson, who served as Mr. Faulkner's confidant, literary agent, and editor early in his career. By the time I met Wasson he was the book editor at the *Delta Democrat-Times* in Greenville, Mississippi.

As fate would have it, when Joseph Blotner's definitive biography of Mr. Faulkner was released, Wasson was in bad health, too ill to review the book. He asked me if I would do the review instead. I considered it an honor to do so. It was during the process of writing that review that I solved a mystery that had long plagued Faulkner scholars. What was the genesis of the writer's creation of his socially and economically challenged family of characters named Snopes?

It was while reading the biography that I realized that Snopes was little more than an anagram for the word peons (with an extra "s" for effect), the term Mr. Faulkner thought most suited his fictional family of low-bred troublemakers, especially when compared to their opposites, the Sartoris family, a representation of Southern landed gentry. That begged the question: from where did he derive the name Sartoris? It could have come from the word sartorial or Sartoria, a community north of Jackson; at the time Sartoris was a common family name in the United States, so he might have just liked the way it sounded; but the most likely source, considering the influences of Native American culture on his writing, was from the Native American word sartoris, which translates to "water that flows over flat land."

"A Rose for Emily" is the first Faulkner story I ever read. It was among the last of the stories he wrote before moving into Rowan Oak. It is a gothic tale that symbolizes the changes taking place in the South. As the old social order decays, leaving Miss Emily and her fine old house in the wake of urban progress, it also reflects the power of a love that sustains resistance, to the very end, of inevitable change, even in the aftermath of death. Speaking at an American Literature seminar at Nagano, Japan, in 1955, Mr. Faulkner explained the story's title: "It was an allegorical title; the meaning was, here was a woman who had had a tragedy, an irrevocable tragedy and nothing could be done about it, and I pitied her and this was a salute ... to a woman you would hand a rose." (source: *Faulkner at Nagano*, ed. Robert Jelliffe).

Although Mr. Faulkner is one of the most revered of American writers, primarily because of the intellectual scope of his fiction, and his often breath-taking writing style, he was not the first author to set a high bar for literary accomplishment in the Triangle. That honor goes to Stark Young, who was born in 1881 in the tiny town of Como, Mississippi, sixteen years before the birth of Mr. Faulkner who wrote several novels before Young published his bestselling antebellum novel *So Red the Rose*, published in 1934, two years before the publication of *Gone With the Wind*.   Not only was Young the Triangle's first bestselling novelist, he was a professor at the University of Mississippi, a translator, and a drama critic, writing for the prestigious *New Republic* and *The New York Times* after leaving the Triangle for New York City. In the mid-1970s a two-volume set of Young's letters came across my desk—and the books were the editorial product of my mentor John Pilkington. The story I chose for *Mojo Rising*, "Jalous Business," came from Young's 1935 book of stories, *Feliciana*. It is set in New Orleans and depicts Creole life and its passionate and sometimes consuming focus on good food.

Eudora Welty's "Why I Live at the P.O." is a flawlessly written story of family pride and emotional instability. This story is one of the reasons that Welty is considered one of America's finest short story writers. She never explains human emotions, the way a lesser writer would do; instead, she shows the reader how emotions dictate behavior and influence feelings. As a reader you quickly forget that the characters are an artificial creation. You accept them as living, breathing entities that could walk off the page, if they were a mind to, and leave you holding a handful of blank pages. Many people consider Welty the finest short story writer ever to have lived.

One of the things I have tried to demonstrate with this collection is to show how writers in the Mojo Triangle have a cultural link not just to the land and its history, but to each other. Just as musicians in the Triangle were inspired to invent new music—blues, jazz, country and rock 'n' roll—so were the region's writers inspired to draw on the power of the Triangle to invent new literary roadmaps and devices to explore the human heart and soul.

With the South as a backdrop, Tennessee Williams delved deeply into human psychology, not just with his Pulitzer Prize-winning dramas but with his short stories that always displayed a unique perspective on the human condition. His story, "Mama's Old Stucco House," originally published in *Esquire* magazine in 1965, is a powerful and haunting glimpse into race relations in the South in situations in which African Americans find themselves as caregivers to white families that find themselves up against the ropes in the final stages of life. Williams's genius is his ability to take the mundane in life and elevate it to high art.

One of the hallmarks of Mojo writing is the irony with which its scribes pursue life. Just as Stark Young could be an educator, an intellectual, and a renowned drama critic at one stage in his life, only to seemingly flip the page to become the author of the Triangle's first bestseller, *So Red the Rose*, which surely inspired Margaret Mitchell to write *Gone With the Wind*, so did Mississippi-born Willie Morris wear different hats in different stages of his career.

A Rhodes Scholar, he studied history at Oxford University before becoming editor of the liberal *Texas Observer*. Willie Morris first showed up on my radar in the mid-to-late 1960s, when he became editor of the influential *Harper's Magazine*. The Vietnam War was raging and civil rights was the issue of the moment. *Harper's* became a beacon of hope for those passionate about ending the war and embracing the civil rights movement. He shocked the magazine world by soliciting articles from some of America's finest writers—William Styron, Norman Mailer, Gay Talese, and David Halberstam. As a result of those efforts, he played a major role in changing and elevating America's literary and journalistic standards.

I first met Willie Morris in the late 1970s while working as a newspaper reporter at the Greenwood (Mississippi) *Commonwealth*. At the time he was promoting his book, *Yazoo: Integration in a Deep-Southern Town*. He told me about a novel

17

he wanted to write that he already had titled *Taps* — *it* was about his experiences as a teenager playing "Taps" for soldiers killed in faraway lands — and a non-fiction book about his friendship with James Jones, author of *From Here to Eternity*. He returned to New York and we kept in touch.

When *James Jones: A Friendship* was published I reviewed it for the *Tallahassee Democrat*, where I was then working as a reporter. I sent Willie a copy of the review, which told the story of how when Jones was in the hospital dying Willie stayed at his side, often sleeping on the floor of the hospital room. Knowing that he was at the end of his life, he asked Willie if he would please finish his work in progress, a novel titled *Whistle.* Willie readily agreed.

Willie responded with a gracious letter (see illustration) which also mentioned his devotion to finishing his novel, *Taps.* We stayed in touch via letters and when he returned to Mississippi in 1980 to be writer-in-residence at the University of Mississippi, I wrote an unsigned editorial welcoming him home in the *Jackson Daily News*, where I was then editorial page editor. Readers were surprised perhaps, that the "most conservative newspaper in America," according to *Time* magazine, would go out on a limb for a liberal wordsmith, but the editorial was approved by editor Jimmy Ward.

Over the years, Willie wrote fewer books about social issues and more about purely human issues. His *My Dog Skip*, which was made into a movie, and *My Cat Spit McGee* (I reviewed it for *BookPage* magazine) are good examples, along with *Good Old Boy: A Delta Boyhood*, also made into a movie for public television. By the time of his unexpected death of a heart attack in 1999, he had become a beloved figure in Mississippi and elsewhere, his earlier liberal viewpoints largely forgotten. I was greatly saddened by his death. Later, I learned that during the precious moments of life following his heart attack he had turned to his wife, JoAnne Prichard Morris, and asked her to "get *Taps* together." It was the same request that Jones had

12/2/79
Bridgehampton

Dear Jim,

I was touched by your splendid review, and impressed also by the writing and the insights.

I showed it to Gloria Jones, who sends you her best.

Best of luck with your writing. Stick with it.

Taps is a ways off, but I feel good about it.

Very best —
Willie Morris

Letter to James L. Dickerson from Willie Morris
Photo from James L. Dickerson Collection

made of him. Willie Morris was a writer to the very end.

Willie died later that day. For most of the following year, JoAnne worked on his manuscript, editing it into its final form, so that it could be published in 2001. When the time came to choose a Willie Morris story for this book, I knew it had to be an excerpt from *Taps*. With the help of his son of a previous marriage, David Rae, and JoAnne, I am able to share a portion of that wonderful book that was thirty years in the making.

Shelby Foote and I share a bond of coincidences. First, we are both natives of Greenville, Mississippi, a river city historically referred to as an oasis of liberalism and literary inclination in a state better known for its lynchings and radical politics. Second, we both worked as reporters for the Pulitzer Prize-winning *Delta Democrat-Times*, when it was owned by the Hodding Carter family. Third, we both migrated to Memphis, Tennessee, where we both lived in Midtown, yet another oasis of civility. The best I can calculate, he wrote his novel, *Love in a Dry Season*, in Greenville, while I, who was much younger, was not yet of school age. When the time came to choose a contribution for this book, I went for a chapter from that novel.

Impeccably written — Shelby, who is best known for his books about the Civil War, began his writing career as a novelist — the book contains much of the subject matter of his Civil War trilogy, which is to say, narrative references to the cultural battles that have become the mainstay of Southern writers, but with an important difference, one a true Mojo dweller could not help but delve into — the murderous consequences of an erotic love triangle. It is a splendid novel, one that moves with the careful dance steps of a well-orchestrated ballet.

When I approached Shelby's literary agent, Scott Gould, about using the chapter in this book, he said he would have to clear it with Shelby's son, Huger. The son's response came quickly — "yes, because that is what father would have wanted." Huger, an internationally known photographer who lives in New York City, also contributed a splendid photograph he took of his father in Paris.

Years later, after my family moved to Hollandale, a small town about eighteen miles from Greenville, the Natchez-born Josephine Ayers Haxton, who lived in Greenville with her husband Kenneth Haxton, a poet and musician of distinction who ran an upscale men's store named Nelms and Blum, wrote a short story that, in part, dealt with the complicated relationships that often existed between black and white Southerners. Titled "On the Lake," the story was published in the August 26, 1961 issue of *The New Yorker*, a magazine that had always looked favorably upon Mojo writers.

A fictionalized account of a boating accident that involved herself, her sons and her former black maid, the story was flawlessly written and made a profound statement about race relations. Not wishing to come under public criticism for her views, she asked *The New Yorker* to publish the story under the pen name of Ellen Douglas. The magazine was not on the stands for long when her cover was blown. Betty Carter, wife of renowned journalist Hodding Carter, recognized the story as being based on a local event. Henceforth, everything Josephine Haxton wrote bore the name Ellen Douglas, although everyone in Mississippi knew it was Mrs. Haxton. She went on to write numerous short stories and eleven books, including *The Rock Cried Out* and *Can't Quit You, Baby*.

I want to thank *The New Yorker* for giving me permission to reprint "On the Lake," one of the few times it has been reprinted—and to her son, Jackson lawyer Ayers Haxton, who consulted with his two brothers, Brooks and Richard, to select a photograph to accompany the story.

The Mojo Triangle has been blessed with strong and creative female writers, beginning with Eudora Welty, of course, but continuing with two other "Masters" included in this anthology—Elizabeth Spencer and Ellen Gilchrist, both of whom are still living at the time of this writing (2017). Ms. Spencer, originally from Carrollton, Mississippi, just outside

Greenwood, currently lives in Chapel Hill, North Carolina. For a time she taught creative writing at the University of North Carolina.

A five-time recipient of the O. Henry Award for her short stories, Ms. Spencer has written seven collections of short stories and nine novels, including *The Voice at the Back Door* and *The Light in the Piazza,* which was made into a movie in 1962 starring Olivia de Havilland and George Hamilton. In 2005 it was made into a very successful Broadway play. Ms. Spencer has lived in Italy, where she married her British-born husband, John Rusher, and Montreal, Canada, where she taught writing at Concordia University. In the mid-1940s she worked as a reporter at the Nashville *Tennessean,* moving on after a couple of years to the University of Mississippi, where she taught English and creative writing.

Choosing between Ms. Spencer's many fine stories for a representative story for this collection was like choosing which sunset is best. In the end, we chose "The Boy in the Tree," a wonderful story about the complicated options family members face when dealing with mental health issues and aging, even when those issues go by names unrelated to mental health. The most common way, of course, is to deny that a problem even exists. The writing of this story smells like freshly planed sandalwood and its clean scent will haunt you for days after you finish it.

Ellen Gilchrist was born in Vicksburg, Mississippi, eventually gravitating to Jackson, where she received a Bachelor of Arts degree in philosophy at Millsaps College and studied creative writing under Eudora Welty at the college. Although it is her short fiction for which she is best known (her collection of stories, *Victory Over Japan,* won the U.S. National Book Award for fiction in 1984), she also has won awards for her poetry. She currently lives in Fayetteville, Arkansas, where she is a professor of creative writing and contemporary fiction at the University of Arkansas.

We are fortunate that Ms. Gilchrist graced us with a previously unpublished story, titled "A Christmas Story," which is being published for the first time in *Mojo Rising*. It is about the Christmas Eve birth of a baby girl in Ocean Springs, Mississippi, an "unasked-for, unintended blessing [that] slid down the birth canal and came out with her eyes wide open." How the family reacts to the birth—and the stories they share on this occasion—are at the heart of this wonderful story. We are also grateful that Ms. Gilchrist selected the photograph we used to introduce her story.

Rounding out our story selection is a short story titled "Big Black Good Man," written by Richard Wright, easily one of the top three African American writers in this country's history. Born in 1908 at a plantation at Roxie Mississippi, just outside Natchez, he was the grandson of slaves. However, Natchez was only a pit-stop in his life's journey. After living in Quebec, Canada, for a while, he moved to Paris in 1946, where he remained until his death in 1960.

While in Paris he befriended French writers such as Jean-Paul Sartre and Albert Camus. He wrote about a dozen novels and short story collections, and an equal number of non-fiction books, most of which dealt with racial issues in the United States. His novel, *Native Son*, played an important role in helping change race relations in the United States. About that book, Jack Miles wrote in the *Los Angeles Times* that the book: "… is central both to an ongoing conversation among African-American writers and critics and to the consciousness among all American readers of what it means to live in a multiracial society in which power splits among racial lines."

"Big Black Good Man" takes place in Copenhagen and tells the story of a giant black, seafaring man who checks into a hotel with a white night clerk who feels an overpowering sense of fear when dealing with the giant black man. The writing in this story is energetic and the plotting presents one surprise after another. The night clerk does not want to feel he is racist, but he has a lingering feeling that he might be. The surprise ending is a powerful one and seems appropriate for an O. Henry ending.

I chose the story because I was mesmerized by the writing and I feel that it is a prime example of the sort of narrative power that only comes from writers associated with the Mojo Triangle. I can promise you that you will think about this story long after you have finished it and moved on to other matters. It is unforgettable, not just because of the intriguing storyline, but because it can't help but remind one of the unfinished business we still have in America when it comes to race relations.

I hope you enjoy reading these stories as much as I did collecting them. They are a reminder of who we are as Mojo Triangle denizens, at least those of us who call it home, and how much America has depended on the Mojo Triangle for much of its greatest literature. And because this is the first time these great writers have been assembled in one book, it serves as a gift to the State of Mississippi which is celebrating its 200th birthday as this book is being published.

—**James L. Dickerson**

Rowan Oak Photo Courtesy Robert Jordan/Ole Miss Communications

William Faulkner   Photo by Carl Van Vechten / Library of Congress

A ROSE FOR EMILY

BY WILLIAM FAULKNER

When Miss Emily Grierson died, our whole town went to her funeral: the men through a sort of respectful affection for a fallen monument, the women mostly out of curiosity to see the inside of her house, which no one save an old manservant — a combined gardener and cook — had seen in at least ten years.

It was a big, squarish house that had once been white, decorated with cupolas and spires and scrolled balconies in the heavily lightsome style of the seventies, set on what had once been our most select street. But garages and cotton gins had encroached and obliterated even the august names of that neighborhood; only Miss Emily's house was left, lifting its stubborn and coquettish decay above the cotton wagons and the gasoline pumps — an eyesore among eyesores. And now Miss Emily had gone to join the representatives of those august names where they lay in the cedar-bemused cemetery among the ranked and anonymous graves of Union and Confederate soldiers who fell at the battle of Jefferson.

Alive, Miss Emily had been a tradition, a duty, and a care; a sort of hereditary obligation upon the town, dating from that day in 1894 when Colonel Sartoris, the mayor — he who fa-thered the edict that no Negro woman should appear on the streets without an apron — remitted her taxes, the dispensation dating from the death of her father on into perpetuity. Not that Miss Emily would have accepted charity. Colonel Sartoris invented an involved tale to the effect that Miss Emily's father had loaned money to the town, which the town, as a matter of business, preferred this way of repaying. Only a man of Colonel Sartoris' generation and thought could have invented it, and only a woman could have believed it.

When the next generation, with its more modern ideas, became mayors and aldermen, this arrangement created some lit-tle dissatisfaction. On the first of the year they mailed her a tax notice. February came, and there was no reply. They wrote her a formal letter, asking her to call at the sheriff's office at her convenience.

A week later the mayor wrote her himself, offering to call or so send his car for her, and received in reply a note on paper of an archaic shape, in a thin, flowing calligraphy in faded ink, to the effect that she no longer went out at all. The tax notice was also enclosed, without comment.

They called a special meeting of the Board of Aldermen. A deputation waited upon her, knocked at the door through which no visitor had passed since she ceased giving china-painting lessons eight or ten years earlier. They were admitted by the old Negro into a dim hall from which a stairway mounted into still more shadow. It smelled of dust and dis-use — a close, dank smell. The Negro led them into the parlor. It was furnished in heavy, leather-covered furniture. When the Negro opened the blinds of one window, they could see that the leather was cracked; and when they sat down, a faint dust rose sluggishly about their thighs, spinning with slow motes in the single sun-ray. On a tarnished gilt easel before the fireplace stood a crayon portrait of Miss Emily's father.

They rose when she entered — a small, fat woman in black, with a thin gold chain descending to her waist and vanishing into her belt, leaning on an ebony cane with a tarnished gold head. Her skeleton was small and spare; perhaps that was why what would have been merely plumpness in another was obesity in her. She looked bloated, like a body long submerged in motionless water, and of that pallid hue. Her eyes, lost in the fatty ridges of her face, looked like two small pieces of coal pressed into a lump of dough as they moved from one face to another while the visitors stated their errand.

She did not ask them to sit. She just stood in the door and listened quietly until the spokesman came to a stumbling halt. Then they could hear the invisible watch ticking at the end of the gold chain.

Her voice was dry and cold. "I have no taxes in Jefferson. Colonel Sartoris explained it to me. Perhaps one of you can gain access to the city records and satisfy yourselves."

"But we have. We are the city authorities, Miss Emily. Didn't you get a notice from the sheriff, signed by him?"

"I received a paper, yes," Miss Emily said. "Perhaps he considers himself the sheriff ... I have no taxes in Jefferson."

"But, Miss Emily — "

"See Colonel Sartoris." (Colonel Sartoris had been dead almost ten years." "I have no taxes in Jefferson, Tobe!" The Negro appeared. "Show these gentlemen out."

* * *

So she vanquished them, horse and foot, just as she had vanquished their fathers thirty years before about the smell. That was two years after her father's death and a short time after her sweetheart — the one we believed would marry her — had deserted her. After her father's death she went out very little; after her sweetheart went away, people hardly saw her at all. A few of the ladies had the temerity to call, but were not received, and the only sign of life about the place was the Negro man — a young man then — going in and out with a market basket.

"Just as if a man — any man — could keep a kitchen properly," the ladies said; so they were not surprised when the smell developed, It was another link between the gross, teeming world and the high and mighty Griersons.

A neighbor, a woman, complained to the mayor, Judge Stevens, eighty years old.

"But what will you have me do about it, madam?" he said.

"Why, send her word to stop it," the woman said. "Isn't there a law?"

"I'm sure that won't be necessary," Judge Stevens said. "It's probably just a snake or a rat that nigger of hers killed in the yard. I'll speak to him about it."

The next day he received two more complaints, one from a man who came in diffident deprecation "We really must do something about it, Judge. I'd be the last one in the world to bother Miss Emily, but we've got to do something." That night, the Board of Aldermen met — three graybeards and one younger man, a member of the rising generation.

"Damnit sir," Judge Stevens said, "will you accuse a lady to her face of smelling bad?"

So the next night, after midnight, four men crossed Miss Emily's lawn and slunk about the house like burglars, sniffing along the base of the brickwork and at the cellar openings while one of them performed a regular sowing motion with his hand out of a sack slung from his shoulder. They broke open the cellar door and sprinkled lime there, and in all the outbuildings. As they recrossed the lawn, a window that had been dark was lighted and Miss Emily sat in it, the light behind her, and her upright torso motionless as that of an idol. They crept quietly across the lawn and into the shadow of the locusts that lined the street. After a week or two the smell went away.

That was when people had begun to feel really sorry for her. People in our town, remembering how old lady Wyatt, her great-aunt, had gone completely crazy at last, believed that the Griersons held themselves a little too high for what they really were. None of the young men were quite good enough for Miss Emily and such. We had long thought of them as a tableau, Miss Emily a slender figure in white in the background, her father a spraddled silhouette in the foreground, his back to her and clutching a horsewhip, the two of them framed by the back-flung front door. So when she got to be thirty and was still single, we were not pleased exactly, but vindicated; even with insanity in the family she wouldn't have turned down all of her chances if they had really materialized.

When her father died, it got about that the house was all that was left to her; and in a way, people were glad. At last they could pity Miss Emily. Being left alone, and a pauper she had become humanized. Now she too would know the old thrill and the old despair of a penny more or less.

The day after his death all the ladies prepared to call at the house and offer condolence and aid, as is our custom. Miss Emily met them at the door, dressed as usual and with no trace of grief on her face. She told them that her father was not dead. She did that for three days, with the ministers calling on her, and the doctors trying to persuade her to let them dispose of the body. Just as they were about to resort to law and force she broke down, and they buried her father quickly.

We did not say she was crazy then. We believed she had to do that. We remembered all the young men her father had driven away, and we knew that with nothing left, she would have to cling to that which had robbed her, as people will.

* * *

She was sick for a long time. When we saw her again, her

hair was cut short, making her look like a girl, with a vague resemblance to those angels in colored church windows — sort of tragic and serene.

The town had just let the contracts for paving the sidewalks, and in the summer after her father's death they began the work. The construction company came with niggers and mules and machinery, and a foreman named Homer Barron, a Yankee — a big, dark, ready man, with a big voice and eyes lighter than his face. The little boys would follow in groups to hear him cuss the niggers, and the niggers singing in time to the rise and fall of picks. Pretty soon he knew everybody in town. Whenever you heard a lot of laughing anywhere about the square, Homer Barron would be in the center of the group. Presently we began to see him and Miss Emily on Sunday afternoons driving in the yellow-wheeled buggy and the matched team of bays from the livery stable.

At first we were glad that Miss Emily would have an interest, because the ladies all said, "Of course a Grierson would not think seriously of a Northerner, a day laborer." But there were still others, older people, who said that even grief could not cause a real lady to forget noblesse oblige — without calling it noblesse oblige. They just said, "Poor Emily. Her kinsfolk should come to her." She had some kin in Alabama; but years ago her father had fallen out with them over the estate of old lady Wyatt, the crazy woman, and there was no communication between the two families. They had not even been represented at the funeral.

And as soon as the old people said, "Poor Emily," the whispering began. "Do you suppose it's really so?" they said to one another. "Of course it is. What else could ..." This behind their hands; rustling of craned silk and satin behind jalousies closed upon the sun of Sunday afternoon as the thin, swift clop-clop-clop of the matched team passed: "Poor Emily."

She carried her head high enough — even when we believed that she was fallen. It was as if she demanded more than ever the recognition of her dignity as the last Grierson; as if it had wanted that touch of earthiness to reaffirm her imperviousness. Like when she bought the rat poison, the arsenic. That was over a year after they had begun to say "Poor Emily," and while the two female cousins were visiting her.

"I want some poison," she said to the druggist. She was over thirty then, still a slight woman, though thinner than usual, with cold, haughty black eyes in a face the flesh of which was strained across the temples and about the eye sockets as you imagine a lighthouse-keeper's face ought to look. "I want some poison," she said.

"Yes, Miss Emily. What kind? For rats and such? I'd recom-
-."

"I want the best you have. I don't care what kind."

The druggist named several. "They'll kill anything up to an elephant. But what you want is — "

"Arsenic," Miss Emily said. "Is that a good one?"

"Is … arsenic? Yes, ma'am. But what you want — "

"I want arsenic."

The druggist looked down at her. She looked back at him, erect, her face like a strained flag. "Why, of course," the druggist said. "If that's what you want. But the law requires you to tell what you are going to use it for."

Miss Emily just stared at him, her head tilted back in order to look him eye for eye, until he looked away and went and got the arsenic and wrapped it up. The Negro delivery boy brought her the package; the druggist didn't come back. When she opened the package at home there was written on the box, under the skull and bones: For rats."

* * *

So the next day we all said, "She will kill herself"; and we said it would be the best thing. When she had first begun to be seen with Homer Barron, we had said "She will marry him."

Then we said, "She will persuade him yet," because Homer himself had remarked — he liked men, and it was known that imperviousness. Like when she bought the rat poison, the arsenic. That was over a year after they had begun to say "Poor he drank with the younger men in the Elks' Club — that he was not a marrying man. Later, we said, "Poor Emily," behind the jalousies as they passed on Sunday afternoon in the glittering buggy, Miss Emily with her head high and Homer Barron with his hat cocked and a cigar in his teeth, reins and whip in a yellow glove.

Then some of the ladies began to say that it was a disgrace to the town and a bad example to the young people. The men did not want to interfere, but at last the ladies forced the Baptist minister — Miss Emily's people were Episcopal — to call upon her. He would never divulge what happened during that interview, but he refused t go back again The next Sunday they again drove about the streets, and the following day the minister's wife wrote to Miss Emily's relations in Alabama.

So she had blood-kin under her roof again and we sat back to watch developments. At first nothing happened. Then we were sure that they were to be married. We learned that Miss Emily had been to the jeweler's and ordered a man's toilet set in silver, with the letters H.B. on each piece. Two days later we learned that she had bought a complete outfit of men's clothing, including a nightshirt, and we said, "They are married." We were really glad. We were glad because the two female cousins were even more Grierson than Miss Emily had ever been.

So we were not surprised when Homer Barron — the streets had been finished some time since — was gone. We were a little disappointed that there was not a public blowing-off, but we believed that he had gone on to prepare for Miss Emily's coming, or to give her a chance to get rid of the cousins. (By that time it was a cabal, and we were all Miss Emily's allies to help circumvent the cousins.) Sure enough, after another week they departed. And as we had expected all along, within three days

Homer Barron was back in town. A neighbor saw the Negro man admit him at the kitchen door at dusk one evening.

And that was the last we saw of Homer Barron. And of Miss Emily for some time. The Negro man went in and out with the market basket, but the front door remained closed. Now and then we would see her at a window for a moment, as the men did that night when they sprinkled the lime, but for almost six months she did not appear on the streets. Then we knew that this was to be expected too; as if that quality of her father which had thwarted her woman's life so many times had been too virulent and too furious to die.

When we next saw Miss Emily, she had grown fat and her hair was turning gray. During the next few years it grew grayer and grayer until it attained an even pepper-and-salt iron-gray, when it ceased turning. Up to the day of her death at seventy-four it was still that vigorous iron-gray, like the hair of an active man.

From that time on her front door remained closed, save for a period of six or seven years, when she was about forty during which she gave lessons in china-painting. She fitted up a studio in one of the downstairs rooms, where the daughters and granddaughters of Colonel Sartoris' contemporaries were sent to her with the same regularity and in the same spirit that they were sent to church on Sundays with a twenty-five-cent piece for the collection plate. Meanwhile her taxes had been remitted.

Then the newer generation became the backbone and the spirit of the town and the painting pupils grew up and fell away and did not send their children to her with boxes of color and tedious brushes and pictures cut from the ladies' magazines. The front door closed upon the last one and remained closed for good. When the town got free postal delivery, Miss Emily alone refused to let them fasten the metal numbers above her door and attach a mailbox to it. She would not listen to them.

Daily, monthly, yearly we watched the Negro grow grayer and more stooped, going in and out with the market basket. Each December we sent her a tax notice, which would be returned by the post office a week later, unclaimed. Now and then we would see her in one of the downstairs windows — she had evidently shut up the top floor of the house — like the carven torso of an idol in a niche, looking in or not looking at us, we could never tell which. Thus she passed from generation to generation — dear, inescapable, impervious, tranquil, and perverse.

And so she died. Fell ill in the house filled with dust and shadows, with only a doddering Negro man to wait on her. We did not even know she was sick; we had long since given up trying to get any information from the Negro. He talked to no one, probably not even to her, for his voice had grown harsh and rusty, as if from disuse.

She died in one of the downstairs rooms, in a heavy walnut bed with a curtain, her gray head propped on a pillow yellow and moldy with age and lack of sunlight.

* * *

The Negro met the first of the ladies at the front door and let them in, with their hushed, sibilant voices and their quick curious glances, and then he disappeared. He walked right through the house and out the back and was not seen again.

The two female cousins came at once They held the funeral on the second day, with the town coming to look at Miss Emily beneath a mass of bought flowers, with the crayon face of her father musing profoundly above the bier and the ladies sibilant and macabre; and the very old men — some in their brushed Confederate uniforms — on the porch and the lawn, talking of Miss Emily as if she had been a contemporary of theirs, believing that they had danced with her and courted her perhaps confusing time with its mathematical progression, as the old do, to whom all the past is not a diminishing road but, instead, a huge meadow which no winter ever quite touches, divided from them now by the narrow bottle-neck of the most recent decade of years.

Already we knew that there was one room in that region above stairs which no one had seen in forty years, and which would have to be forced. They waited until Miss Emily was decently in the ground before they opened it.

The violence of breaking down the door seemed to fill this room with pervading dust. A thin, acrid pall as of the tomb seemed to lie everywhere upon this room decked and furnished as for a bridal: upon the valance curtains of faded rose color, upon the rose-shaded lights, upon the dressing table, upon the delicate array of crystal and the man's toilet things backed with tarnished silver, silver so tarnished that the monogram was obscured Among them lay a collar and tie as if they had just been removed, which, lifted, left upon the surface a pale crescent in the dust. Upon a chair hung the suit, carefully folded; beneath it the two mute shoes and the discarded socks.

The man himself lay in the bed.

For a long time while we just stood there, looking down at the profound and fleshless grin. The body had apparently once lain in the attitude of an embrace, but now the long sleep that outlasts love, that conquers even the grimace of love, had cuckolded him. What was left of him, rotted beneath what was left of the nightshirt, had become inextricable from the bed in which he lay; and upon him and upon the pillow beside him lay that even coating of the patient and biding dust.

Then we noticed that in the second pillow was the indentation of a head. One of us lifted something from it, and leaning forward, that faint and invisible dust dry and acrid in the nostrils, we saw a long strand of iron-gray hair.

* * *

William Faulkner, (1897 – 1962), one of America's most celebrated writers of fiction, was born in New Albany, Mississippi, a small community not far from Oxford, Mississippi, which he later called home for most of his life. He was the recipient of the 1949 Nobel Prize in Literature and two Pulitzer Prize awards for his novels *A Fable* and *The Reivers*. His novels *The Sound and the Fury* and *As I Lay Dying* are generally regarded as the best English-language novels of the 20th Century.

Eudora Welty (1980) Photo with thanks to Mary Alice Welty White
Photo by Robert Williams, courtesy Mississippi Department
of Archives and History

WHY I LIVE AT THE P.O.

BY EUDORA WELTY

I was getting along fine with Mama, Papa-Daddy and Uncle Rondo until my sister Stella-Rondo just separated from her husband and came back home again. Mr. Whitaker! Of course I went with Mr. Whitaker first, when he first appeared in China Grove, taking "Pose Yourself" photos, and Stella-Rondo broke us up. Told him I was one sided. Bigger on one side than the other, which is a deliberate, calculated falsehood: I'm the same. Stella-Rondo is exactly twelve months to the day younger than I am and for that reason she's spoiled.

She's always had anything in the world she wanted and then she'd throw it away. Papa-Daddy gave her this gorgeous Add-a-Pearl necklace when she was eight years old and she threw it away playing baseball when she was nine, with only two pearls.

So as soon as she got married and moved away from home the first thing she did was separate! From Mr. Whitaker! This photographer with the popeyes she said she trusted. Came home from one of those towns up in Illinois and to our complete surprise brought this child of two.

Mama said she like to made her drop dead for a second. "Here you had this marvelous blonde child and never so much as wrote your mother a word about it," says Mama. "I'm thoroughly ashamed of you." But of course she wasn't.

Stella-Rondo just calmly takes off this hat, I wish you could see it. She says, "Why, Mama, Shirley-T's adopted, I can prove it."

"How?" says Mama, but all I says was, "H'm!" There I was over the hot stove, trying to stretch two chickens over five people and a completely unexpected child into the bargain, without one moment's notice.

"What do you mean—'H'm!'?" says Stella-Rondo, and Mama says, "I heard that, Sister."

I said that oh, I didn't mean a thing, only that whoever Shirley-T. was, she was the spit-image of Papa-Daddy if he'd cut off his beard, which of course he'd never do in the world. Papa-Daddy's Mama's papa and sulks.

Stella-Rondo got furious! She said, "Sister, I don't need to tell you you got a lot of nerve and always did have and I'll thank you to make no future reference to my adopted child whatsoever."

"Very well," I said. "Very well, very well. Of course I noticed at once she looks like Mr. Whitaker's side too....... That frown. She looks like a cross between Mr. Whitaker and Papa-Daddy."

"Well, all I can say is she isn't."

"She looks exactly like Shirley Temple to me," says Mama, but Shirley-T. just ran away from her.

So the first thing Stella-Rondo did at the table was turn Papa-Daddy against me.

"Papa-Daddy," she says. He was trying to cut up his meat. "Papa-Daddy!" I was taken completely by surprise. Papa-Daddy is about a million years old and's got this long-long beard. "Papa-Daddy Sister says she fails to understand why

41

you don't cut off your beard."

So Papa-Daddy l-a-y-s down his knife and fork! He's real rich. Mama says he is, he says he isn't. So he says, "Have I heard correctly? You don't understand why I don't cut off my beard?"

"Why," I says. "Papa-Daddy, of course I understand, I did not say any such of a thing, the idea!"

He says, "Hussy!"

I says, "Papa-Daddy, you know I wouldn't any more want you to cut off your beard than the man in the moon. It was the farthest thing from my mind! Stella-Rondo sat there and made that up while she was eating breast of chicken."

But he says, "So the postmistress fails to understand why I don't cut off my beard. Which job I got you through my influence with the government. "Bird's nest — is that what you call it?"

Not that it isn't the next to smallest P.O. in the entire state of Mississippi.

I says, "Oh, Papa-Daddy," I says, "I didn't say any such of a thing, I never dreamed it was a bird's nest, I have always been grateful though this is the next to smallest P.O. in the state of Mississippi, and I do not enjoy being referred to as a hussy by my own grandfather."

But Stella-Rondo says, "Yes, you did say it too. Anybody in the world could of heard you, that had ears."

"Stop right there," says Mama, looking at *me*.

So I pulled my napkin straight back through the napkin ring and left the table.

As soon as I was out of the room, Mama says, "Call her back, or she'll starve to death," but Papa-Daddy says, "This is the beard I started growing on the Coast when I was fifteen years old." He would of gone on till nightfall if Shirley-T. hadn' lost the Milky Way she ate in Cairo.

So Papa-Daddy says, "I am going out and lie in the hammock, and you can all sit here and remember my words. I'll never cut off my beard as long as I live, even one inch, and I don't appreciate it in you at all." Passed right by me in the hall and went straight out and got in the hammock.

It would be a holiday. It wasn't five minutes before Uncle Rondo suddenly appeared in the hall in one of Stella-Rondo's flesh-colored kimonos, all cut on the bias, like something Mr. Whitaker probably thought was gorgeous.

"Uncle Rondo!" I says. "I didn't know who that was! Where are you going?"

"Sister," he says, "get out of my way, I'm poisoned."

"If you're poisoned stay away from Papa-Daddy," I says. "Keep out of the hammock Papa-Daddy will certainly beat you on the head if you come within forty miles of him. He thinks I deliberately said he ought to cut off his beard after he got me the P.O., and I've told him and told him and told him, and he acts like he just don't hear me. Papa-Daddy must of gone stone deaf."

"He picked a fine day to do it then," says Uncle Rondo, and before you could say "Jack Robinson" flew out in the yard.

What he'd really done, he'd drunk another bottle of that prescription. He does it every single Fourth of July as sure as shooting, and it's horribly expensive. Then he falls over in the hammock and snores. So he insisted on zigzagging right on out to the hammock, looking like a half-wit.

Papa-Daddy woke up with this horrible yell and right there without moving an inch he tried to turn Uncle Rondo against me. I heard every word he said. Oh, he told Uncle Rondo I didn't learn to read till I was eight years old and he didn't see how in the world I ever got the mail put up at the P.O., much less read it all, and he said if Uncle Rondo could not fathom the lengths he had gone to to get me that job! And he said on the other hand he thought Stella-Rondo had a brilliant mind and deserved credit for getting out of town. All the time he was just lying there swinging as pretty as you please and looping out his beard, and poor Uncle Rondo was *pleading* with him to slow down the hammock, it was making him as dizzy as a witch to watch it. But that's what Papa-Daddy likes about a hammock. So Uncle Rondo was too dizzy to get turned against me for the time being. He's Mama's only brother and is a good case of a one-track mind. Ask anybody. A certified pharmacist.

Just then I heard Stella-Rondo raising the upstairs window. While she was married she got this peculiar idea that it's cooler with the windows shut and locked. So she has to raise the window before she can make a soul hear her outdoors.

So she raises the window and says, "*Oh!*" You would have thought she was mortally wounded.

Uncle Rondo and Papa-Daddy didn't even look up, but kept right on with what they were doing. I had to laugh.

I flew up the stairs and threw the door open! I says, "What in the wide world's the matter, Stella-Rondo? You mortally wounded?"

"No," she says, "I am not mortally wounded but I wish you would do me the favor of looking out that window there and telling me what you see."

So I shade my eyes and look out the window.

"I see the front yard," I says.

"Don't you see any human beings?" she says.

"I see Uncle Rondo trying to run Papa-Daddy out of the hammock," I says. "Nothing more. Naturally, it's so suffocating-hot in the house, with all the windows shut and locked, everybody who cares to stay in their right mind will have to go out and get in the hammock before the Fourth Of July is over."

"Don't you notice anything different about Uncle Rondo?" asks Stella-Rondo.

"Why, no, except he's got on some terrible-looking flesh-colored contraption I wouldn't be found dead in, is all I can say," I says.

"Never mind, you won't be found dead in it, because it happens to be part of my trousseau,, and Mr. Whitaker took several dozen photographs of me in it," says Stella-Rondo.

"What on earth could Uncle Rondo *mean* by wearing part of my

trousseau out in the board open daylight without saying so
much as 'Kiss my foot,' *knowing* I only got home this morning
after my separation and hung my negligee up on the bathroom
door, just as nervous as I could be?"

"I'm sure I don't know, and what do you expect me to do
about it?" I says. "Jump out the window?"

"No, I expect nothing of the kind. I simply declare that Uncle Rondo looks like a fool in it, that's all," she says. "It makes
me sick to my stomach."

"Well, he looks as good as he can," I says. "As good as anybody in reason could." I stood up for Uncle Rondo, please remember. And I said to Stella Rondo, "I think I would do well
not to criticize so freely if I were you and came home with a
two-year-old child I had never said a word about, and no explanation whatever about my separation."

"I asked you the instant I entered this house not to refer one
more time to my adopted child, and you gave me your word of
honor you would not," was all Stella-Rondo would say, and
started pulling out every one of her eyebrows with some cheap
Kress tweezers.

So I merely slammed the door behind me and went down
and made some green-tomato pickle. Somebody had to do it.
Of course Mama had turned both the niggers loose; she always
said no earthly power could hold one anyway on the Fourth of
July, so she wouldn't even try It turned out that Japan fell in the
lake and came within a very narrow limit of drowning.

So Mama trots in. Lifts up the lid and says, "H'm! Not very
good for your Uncle Rondo in his precarious condition, I must
say. Or poor little adopted Shirley-T. Shame on you!"

That made me tired. I says, "Well, Stella-Rondo had better
thank her lucky stars it was her instead of me came trotting in
with that very peculiar-looking child. Now if it had been me
that trotted in from Illinois and brought a peculiar-looking
child of two, I shudder to think of the reception I'd of got, much
less controlled the diet of an entire family."

"But you must remember, Sister, that you were never married to Mr. Whitaker in the first place, and didn't go up to Illinois to live," says Mama, shaking a spoon in my face. "If you had I would have been just as overjoyed to see you and your little adopted girl as I was to see Stella-Rondo, when you wound up with your separation and came on back home."

"You would not," I says.

"Don't contradict me, I would," says Mama.

But I said she couldn't convince me though she talked till she was blue in the face. Then I said, "Besides, you know as well as I do that that child is not adopted."

"She most certainly is adopted," says Mama, stiff as a poker.

I says, "Why Mama, Stella-Rondo had her just as sure as anything in this world, and just too stuck up to admit it."

"Why, Sister," said Mama. "Here I thought we were going to have a pleasant Fourth of July, and you start right out not believing a word your own baby sister tells you."

"Just like Cousin Annie Flo. Went to her grave denying the facts of life," I remind Mama.

"I told you if you ever mentioned Annie Flo's name I'd slap your face," says Mama, and slaps my face.

"All right, you wait and see," I says.

"I," says Mama. "*I* prefer to take my children's word for anything when it's humanly possible."

You ought to see Mama, she weighs two hundred pounds and has real tiny feet.

Just then something perfectly horrible occurred to me.

"Mama," I says, "can that child talk?" I simply had to whisper. "Mama, I wonder if that child can be — you know — in any way? Do you realize," I says, "that she hasn't spoken one single, solitary word to a human being up to this minute? This is the way she looks," I says, and I looked like this.

Well, Mama and I just stood there and stared at each other. It was horrible!

"I remember well that Joe Whitaker frequently drank like a fish," says Mama. "I believed to my soul he drank chemicals." And without another word she marches to the foot of the stairs and calls for Stella Rondo.

"Stella-Rondo? O-o-o-o-o! Stella-Rondo!"

"What?" says Stella-Rondo from upstairs. Nor even the grace to get up off the bed.

"Can that child of yours talk" asks Mama.

Stella-Rondo says, "Can she what?"

"Talk! Talk!" says Mama. "Burdyburdyburdyburdy!"

So Stella-Rondo yells back, "Who says she can't talk!"

"Sister says so," says Mama.

"You didn't have to tell me, I know whose word of honor don't mean a thing in this house," says Stella-Rondo.

And in a minute the loudest Yankee voice I ever heard in my life yells out, "OE'm Pop-OE the Sailor-r-r-r Ma-a-an!" and then somebody jumps up and down in the upstairs hall. In another second the house would of fallen down.

"Not only talks, she can tap-dance!" calls Stella-Rondo. "Which is more than some people I won't I won't name can do."

"Why, the little precious darling thing!" Mama says, so surprised. "Just as smart as she can be!" Starts talking baby talk right there. Then she turns on me. "Sister, you ought to be thoroughly ashamed! Run upstairs this instant and apologize to Stella-Rondo and Shirley-T."

"Apologize for what?" I says. "I merely wondered if the child was normal, that's all. Now that she's proved she is, why, I have nothing further to say."

But Mama just turned her heel and flew out, furious. She ran right upstairs and hugged the baby. She believed it was adopted. Stella-Rondo hadn't done a thing but turn her against me from upstairs while I stood there helpless over the hot stove. So that made Mama, Papa-Daddy and the baby all on Stella-Rondo's side.

Next, Uncle Rondo.

I must say that Uncle Rondo has been marvelous to me at various times in the past and I was completely unprepared to be made to jump out of my skin, the way it turned out. Once Stella-rondo did something perfectly horrible to him—broke a chain letter from Flanders Field—and he took the radio back he had given her and gave it to me. Stella-Rondo was furious! For six months we all had to call her Stella instead of Stella-Rondo, or she wouldn't answer. I always thought Uncle Rondo had all the brains of the entire family. Another time he sent me to Mammoth Cave, with all expenses paid.

But this would be the day he was drinking that prescription, the Fourth of July.

So at supper Stella-Rondo speaks up and says she thinks Uncle Rondo ought to try to eat a little something. So finally Uncle Rondo said he would try to eat a little cold biscuits and ketchup, but that was all. So *she* brought it to him.

"Do you think it wise to disport with ketchup in Stella-Rondo's flesh-colored kimono?" I says. Trying to be considerate! If Stella-Rondo couldn't watch out for her trousseau, somebody had to.

"Any objections?" asks Uncle Rondo, just about to pour out all the ketchup.

"Don't mind what she says, Uncle Rondo," says Stella-Rondo. "Sister has been devoting this solid afternoon to sneering out my bedroom window at the way you look."

"What's that?" says Uncle Rondo. Uncle Rondo has got the most terrible temper in the world. Anything is liable to make him tear the house down if it comes at the wrong time.

So Stella-Rondo says, "Sisters says, 'Uncle Rondo certainly does look like a fool in the pink kimono!'"

Do you remember who it was really said that?

Uncle Rondo spills out all the ketchup and jumps out of his chair and tears off the kimono and throws it down on the dirty floor and puts his foot on it. It had to be sent all the way to Jackson to the cleaners and re-pleated.

"So that's your opinion of our Uncle Rondo, is it?" he says. "I look like a fool, do I? Well, that's the last straw. A while day in this house with nothing to do, and then to hear you come out with a remark like that behind my back!"

"I didn't say any such of a thing, Uncle Rondo," I says, "and I'm not saying who did, either. Why, I think you look all right. Just try to take care of yourself and not talk and eat at the same time," I says. "I think you better go lie down."

"Lie down my foot," says Uncle Rondo.

I ought to of known by that he was fixing to do something perfectly horrible.

So he didn't do anything that night in the precarious state he was in—just played Casino with Mama and Stella-Rondo and Shirley-T and gave Shirley-T. a nickel with a head on both sides. It tickled her nearly to death, and she called him "Papa." But at 6:30 A.M. the next morning, he threw a whole five-cent package of some unsold one-inch firecrackers from the store as hard as he could into my bedroom and they every one went off. Not one bad one in the string. Anybody else, there'd be one that wouldn't go off.

Well, I'm just terribly susceptible to noise of any kind, the doctor has always told me I was the most sensitive person he had ever seen in his whole life, and I was simply prostrated. I couldn't eat! People tell me they heard it as far as the cemetery, and old Aunt Jep Patterson, that had been holding her own so good, thought it was Judgement Day and she was going to meet her whole family. It's usually so quiet here.

And I'll tell you it didn't take me any longer than a minute to make up my mind what to do. There I was with the whole entire house on Stella-Rondo's side and turned against me. If I have anything at all I have pride.

So I just decided I'd go straight down to the P.O. There's plenty of room there in the back, I says to myself.

Well! I made no bones about letting the family catch on to what I was up to. I didn't try to conceal it.

The first thing they knew, I marched in where they were all playing Old Maid and pulled the electric oscillating fan out by the plug, and everything got real hot. Next I snatched the pillow I'd done the needlepoint on right off the davenport from behind Papa-Daddy. He went ,"Ugh!" I beat Stella-Rondo up the stairs and finally found my charm bracelet in her bureau drawer under a picture of Nelson Eddy.

"So that's the way the land lies," says Uncle Rondo. There he was, piecing on the ham. "Well, Sister, I'll be glad to donate my army cot if you got any place to set it up, providing you'll leave right this minute and let me get some peace." Uncle Rondo was in France.

"Thank you kindly for the cot and 'peace' is hardly the word I would select if I had to resort to firecrackers at 6:30 A.M. in a young girl's bedroom," I says to him. "And as to where I intend to go, you seem to forget my position as postmistress of China Grove, Mississippi," I says. "I've always got the P.O."

Well that made them all sit up and take notice.

I went out front and started digging up some four-o'clocks to plant around the P.O.

"Ah-ah-ah!" says Mama, raising the window. "Those happen to be my four-o-clocks. Everything planted in that star is mine. I've never known you to make anything grow in your life."

"Very well," I says. "But I take the fern. Even you, Mama, can't stand there and deny that I'm the one watered that fern. And I happen to know where I can send in a box top and get a packet of one thousand mixed seeds, no two the same kind, free."

"Oh, where?" Mama wants to know.

But I says, "Two late. You 'tend to our house, and I'll 'tend to mine. You hear things like that all the time if you know how to listen to the radio. Perfectly marvelous offers. Get anything you want free."

So I hope to tell you I marched in and got that radio, and

they could of all bit a nail in two especially Stella-Rondo, that it used to belong to, and she well knew she couldn't get it back, I'd sue for it like a shot. And I very politely took the sewing-machine motor I helped pay the most on to give Mama for Christmas back in 1929, and a good big calendar, with the first-aid remedies on it The thermometer and the Hawaiian ukulele certainly were rightfully mine, and I stood on the step-ladder and got all my watermelon-rind preserves and every fruit and vegetable I'd put up, every jar. Then I began to pull the tacks out of the bluebird wall vases on the archway to the dining room.

"Who told you you could have those, Miss Priss?" says Mama, fanning as hard as she could.

"I bought 'em and I'll keep track of 'em," I says. "I'll tack 'em up one on each side the post-office window, and you can see 'em when you come to ask me for your mail, if you're so dead to see 'em."

"Not I! I'll never darken the door to that post office again if I live to be a hundred," Mama says. "Ungrateful child! After all the money we spent on you at the Normal."

"Me either," says Stella-Rondo. "You can just let my mail lie there and *rot*, for all I care. I'll never come and relieve you of a single, solitary piece."

"I should worry," I says. "And who you think's going to sit down and write you all those big fat letters and postcards, by the way? Mr. Whitaker? Just because he was the only man ever dropped down in China Grove and you got him — unfairly — is he going to sit down and write you a lengthy correspondence after you come home giving no rhyme nor reason whatsoever for your separation and no explanation for the presence of that child? I may not have your brilliant mind, but I fail to see it."

So Mama says, "Sister, I've told you a thousand times that Stella-Rondo simply got homesick, and this child is far too big to be hers," and she says, "Now, why don't you all just sit down and play Casino?"

Then Shirley-T. sticks out her tongue at me in this perfectly horrible way. She has no more manners than the man in the moon. I told her she was going to cross her eyes like that some day and they'd stick."

"It's too late to stop me now," I says. "You should have tried that yesterday. I'm going to the P.O. and the only way you can possibly see me is to visit me there."

So Papa-Daddy says, "You'll never catch me setting foot in that post office, even if I should take a notion into my head to write a letter some place." He says, "I won't have you reachin' out of that little old window with a pair of shears and cuttin' off any beard of mine. I'm too smart for you!"

"We all are," says Stella-Rondo.

But I said, "If you're so smart, where's Mr. Whitaker?"

So then Uncle Rondo says, "I'll thank you from now on to stop reading all the orders I get on postcards and telling everybody in China Grove what you think is the matter with them," but I says, "I draw my own conclusions and will continue in the future to draw them." I says, "If people want to write their inmost secrets on penny postcards, there's nothing in the wide world you can do about it, Uncle Rondo."

"And if you think we'll ever *write* another postcard you're sadly mistaken," says Mama.

"Cutting off your nose to spite your face then," I says. "But if you're all determined to have no more to do with the U.S. mail, think of this: What will Stella-Rondo do now, if she wants to tell Mr. Whitaker to come after her?"

"Wah!" says Stella-Rondo. I knew she'd cry. She had a conniption fit right there in the kitchen.

"It will be interesting to see how long she holds out," I says. "And now — I am leaving."

"Good-by," says Uncle Rondo.

"Oh, I declare," says Mama. "To think that a family of mine should quarrel on the Fourth of July, or the day after, over Stella-Rondo leaving old Mr. Whitaker and having the sweetest

52

little adopted child! It looks like we'd all be glad!"

"Wah!" says Stella-Rondo, and has a fresh conniption fit.

"*He* left *her*—you mark my word," I says. "That's Mr. Whitaker. I know Mr. Whitaker. After all, I knew him first. I said from the beginning he'd up and leave her. I foretold every single thing that's happened."

"Where did he go?" asks Mama.

"Probably to the North Pole, if he knows what's good for him," I says.

But Stella-Rondo just bawled and wouldn't say another word. She flew to her room and slammed the door.

"Now look what you've gone and done, Sister," says Mama. "You go apologize."

"I haven't got time, I'm leaving," I says.

"Well, what are you waiting around for?" asks Uncle Rondo.

So I just picked up the kitchen clock and marched off, without saying "Kiss my foot" or anything and never did tell Stella-Rondo good-by.

There was a nigger girl going along on a little wagon right in front.

"Nigger girl," I says, "come help me haul these things down the hill, I'm going to live in the post office."

Took her nine trips in her express wagon. Uncle Rondo came out on the porch and threw her a nickel.

* * *

And that's the last I've laid eyes on any of my family or my family laid eyes on me for five solid days and nights. Stella-Rondo may be telling the most horrible tales in the world about Mr. Whitaker, but I haven't heard them. As I tell everybody, I draw my own conclusions.

But oh, I like it here. It's ideal, as I've been saying. You see, I've got everything cater-cornered, the way I like it. Hear the radio? All the war news. Radio, sewing machine, book ends, ironing board and that great big piano lamp — peace, that's what I like. Butter-bean vines planted all along the front where the strings are.

Of course, there's not much mail. My family are naturally the main people in China Grove, and if they prefer to vanish from the face of the earth, for all the mail they get or the mail they write, why, I'm not going to open my mouth. Some of the folks here in town are taking up for me and some turned against me LI know which is which. There are always people who will quit buying stamps just to get on the right side of Papa-Daddy.

But here I am, and here I'll stay. I want the world to know I'm happy.

And if Stella-Rondo should come to me this minute, on bended knees, and *attempt* to explain the incidents of her life with Mt Whitaker, I'd simply put my fingers in both my ears and refuse to listen.

* * *

Eudora Welty (1909 – 2001) was born in Jackson, Mississippi, and lived there for most of her life. She attended Mississippi State College for Women, the University of Wisconsin, and the Columbia University School of Business, where she learned to type. Around the time she was graduated from high school, her family moved to a house at 1119 Pinehurst Street, which was her permanent address until her death. The Revival style home is now known as the Eudora Welty House and has been opened for guided tours by the Eudora Welty Foundation.

The author of numerous novels – she was the recipient of a Pulitzer Prize for Fiction in 1973 for her novel *The Optimist's Daughter*, which the *Washington Post* compared to *War and Peace* and *The Tempest* — she was considered by many to reside at the pinnacle of America's short story writers. Other books include *Losing Battles*, *A Curtain of Green* and *The Ponder Heart*, *which earned her the Howells Medal for Fiction by the American Academy of Arts and Letters.*

Stark Young   **Library of Congress**

JALOUS BUSINESS

BY STARK YOUNG

The train arrives at New Orleans at 7:35, and my friend W — is there to meet me. He is a brilliant painter, but it is possible that living for most of the time in a plantation house with a garden does not make one want to paint pictures steadily; life may seem important otherwise.

The truth is he has come to the station to meet me at such an hour because his aunt, Mrs. T--, is afraid that I will get the wrong coffee. She is past eighty, but, like a great Louisiana lady, still thinks food an art.

When we have had the coffee, it turns out that my plans for going to the library on a bit of historical research must first be adjusted to the business of getting the terrapin for the soup that night. His aunt is giving me a dinner, and we must not delay in going to the one place in New Orleans where she gets her terrapin. Then later on, while we are at the library, Roy, the chauffeur, can carry the terrapin home and Theophile, the butler, will put it in the ice-box.

Half way down the long line of the street, the two-story

white house, with its green shuttered doors and tall oleanders growing by the steps, is the terrapin man's. Roy draws the bell-pull, opens for himself the shutter doors, and presently the front door opens to him. He enters as if going into a salon. After a while he comes out with his cool parcel as if emerging from a cave. Now W — and I can go to the library, Roy to Theophile and Celimene.

There is, however, a slight delay. A friend of W — 's has some photographs that I must stop and see, of the plantation houses. Before we know it, an hour has passed. Can you imagine, W — says to me, what Tante is going to think of this riding about with the terrapin for so long? So we decide that he should telephone and say that it will soon arrive and to tell Celimene not to get in a swivet about it. Celimene has been his aunt's cook for many years, so W — tells me; though the place I know the name best is in Moliere, that most chic of all his heroines.

It turns out, from the telephoning, that Mrs. T — is not entirely happy about my lunch. I am to dine with her this evening; that, of course, is settled, and Celimene is very busy. Nevertheless lunch cannot be denied as a fact; and Mrs. T — does not like to think of me eating almost anywhere. W — must bring me out to her house if only for a little while. Celimene can at least stop to make me some *oreilles de cochons*.

Be sure, W — says, to ask after Celimene, and I say I will; for of course I know that the great Creole tradition of a gentleman may include compliments to the cook on the dinner's perfection.

I, naturally, salute first Mrs. T — on my arrival, and try to grace the moment with the pleasures of memory: some years ago we met when I was motoring in the parishes along the Bayou Teche. She has one of the most adorable houses in Louisiana, more than a hundred years old, with a white camellia garden into whose oblong fountain-pool little lead statues look down. And behind the house the stone terrace runs to the bayou, where there is a lattice pa billion to sit in, if you like, on summer evenings, and where you will find the landing for the steamboat that comes up from New Orleans Tuesday and you arrive Friday; the fare, I believe, is $7.

Meanwhile my coat is being deftly taken from me by brown hands. I say auspiciously: "And where is Celimene?"

"This is *moi*," a soft voice says behind me. "this is Celimene."

"Yes, this is Celimene, she is making your *oreilles de cochons* for you. Run, Celimene."

"*Oui, madame.*"

Presently we are in the drawing room, with my hostess on the rosewood sofa and me facing her in the armchair. W — keeps pacing about — he has risen very early for a Louisiana young gentleman.

We talk for a little while on Louisiana and the old days, and something of the cooking in the great Creole houses. But this cannot last long; perhaps, Mrs. T — says, I prefer to see what is going on in the kitchen. W — will take me, yes? Her dear nephew, why will he stay so much in their country place, away from her?

As I pass down the hall I see into the dining-room where the table is laid for dinner that night — laid already, there is more than enough to do for the rest of the day. I have a faint impression of portraits looking down from the wall, stiff, proper, and elegant, One of them has a long nose, one lace, one high stays.

But my eye is drawn most to the table. What with the old silver plates and candlesticks, there will be plenty of light falling on the camellias covering the centre of the table, fifty or sixty, shell-pink and white, white and shell-pink, that have been brought in from the garden in the country. I glanced at the table again as we pass on; and smile to think how those wide plates and candles and flowers for the dinner this evening are like an overture to an orchestra. At least in this house I feel sure they are so.

Meanwhile, I gather, from a certain delicate suspense in the air that, though it is plainly past the hour, I am to be served some sort of lunch. And this is confirmed by W — 's whispering to me on the way to the kitchen that Tante and Celimene have decided that a tray even, is better than wandering about town.

In the kitchen Celimene is making *oreilles de cochons*. She keeps lifting the thin piece of dough and dropping it into the deep fat, then for a moment stands, as it were, fingering the tone of the brown before she gives it the whirl with a fork that will make the pig's ear right. Then while it is hot, she adds the sprinkle of powdered sugar.

I say to Celimene that she must give me the recipe for those delicious looking things.

She will do it, she says, with great pleasure.

W — bursts into a laugh.

"Nothing, all you have to do is to watch it, sir, till it browns *justement*," Celimene tells me, leaning over intently, as she twirls one of the pieces. "Theophile," she says to W--, "has not come with the oysters."

He smiles at me as if to say, now you know exactly how to make *oreilles de cochons*. "And what about the iced water in them, Celimene?" he says; and we turn to go back to the drawing-room, where his aunt is still sitting on the sofa.

Presently a lunch is served me on an old tray whose silver is worn thin at the edges. The lunch is a matter of toasted rolls and fried oysters, black coffee and one or two other things, not sparse.

"You are interested in cooking?" my hostess says to me, as I begin my lunch.

From the onslaught I am making she has a right to think so, but I know what she means. She means that her general impression of me is that I am civilized, which pleases me of course.

In so far as I have time to think of it at all, I say, I am very much interested. In New York we are not unfriendly to cooking, but we are very busy.

I mean this for a *jeu d'esprit*, but it is lost on her.

"Even our young people here, it seems from what I hear, would as soon eat in restaurants,: Mrs. T — goes on, "now did you ever!"

"So?"

"Naturally, I always say when one tells me this, if that be the case, it's quite as good as they deserve."

This time I say, "Indeed?" in the most solemn manner, hoping thus to escape being classed by her as a transient, someone who might be in a mere hotel.

"Not," she goes on, "that some of the places mentioned in the *Gourmet's Guide* are not choice. Antoines, for example, Jules Alciatore, who as a youth made pate de foie gras for Bismark — since Mr. Jefferson, our own statesmen have never seemed to mind food one way or the other — or there's Arnaud's, or Robert and Joseph Cesar, or that famous bisque at the Galatoire brothers."

"But," I say, tactfully, "one's own kitchen — "

"Yes, my dear," she smiles, waving slightly her fragile hand with its old diamonds.

"Do you know" she says, "I hear that now, these days, people eat canned terrapin soup?"

"Do they?" I say, astounded (having eaten it often, not without relish).

The beautiful old eyes are looking gravely at me, as she goes on to speak of cooking in other parts of our country. Now, if you take Kentucky, she says, those people never have known what they wanted; just see what they call fried chicken Tis really only a sort of fricassee, good in its way, she supposes. In

Virginia, it seems, they roast meats quite well. In Maryland, fish or game, ah well--. In my state, Mississippi, they at least use black pepper, which is better than that white pepper up North; which is no better than fly blister. Here in Louisiana they use green peppers, which, of course, makes all the difference. Yes, Southern cooking is the best. (She means Louisiana Creole cooking, but I do not dispute the matter).

None of those places, she goes on, gets enough flavor into food. And, then, you see, in New York there are so many things out of season, take pompano; of course pompano, if one knows, is good only a very short time out of the year. Nobody wants things that have been stacked away in icehouses. Things should be in season.

Meanwhile I have finished my luncheon and drained the last drop of the coffee; and Mrs. T – has risen to go and fetch a jar of the orange preserves that I must taste; she will send me some jars of it to New York, she says.

When she has gone, W — tells me of his aunt's last visit to New York, some years ago. They took a suite for her in one of the hotels near the theatres, and a friend in New York arranged for seats at twenty of the theatre performances. But after a week his aunt said to Celimene, I'm going home." She could not eat the food. "You give me five dollars, madame," said Cellimene. She went to Harlem, where she had a friend who had once been a cook for a good New Orleans family and later had married a Pullman porter. After a time she came back with a lard can of gumbo, and she and her mistress sat down in the drawing-room of the suite and ate it. Then they remained several days longer in New York.

"This preserves," Mrs. T — said, returning with a compote, "I always get the oranges for it at the same place every season. We used to have plenty of them in Louisiana, but the cold weather and floods have killed the trees, all except on this one bayou where I send. They were brought here first from

Andalusia in the Spanish days. It takes two weeks to make it, but I hope you will like it."

I try to eat as daintily as may be some of the preserves, then I pause, mentioning that divine texture, that aroma that is almost sinful — if not sinful, certainly pagan. I remember a portion at least of that aroma when I was a child: vanilla beans have been somehow used. This pleases Mrs. T--, and again she compliments me, mentioning in the same breath some of the bottled concoctions of so-called vanilla.

"Do you know," she goes on presently, "we have a literary friend in Chicago who dined with us here once, and we sent her a few jars of this. In return she sent us some sort of affair made of pears — you could see she had used that confectioner's sugar on it. Of course we didn't eat it. She made a great mistake, I thought; it was quite enough to have sent us one of her delight-ful letters."

She would be delighted to give me some of her recipes, Mrs. T — says, remembering to add, charmingly, that she is sure my servant could make them with success. I am coming to din-ner tonight, but when to Louisiana again? As the Acadians say, when they want you to come again, "You know de road."

Of late years she has given some of her recipes to a number of friends who seem to care for them. These recipes have some down to the fourth generation in her family, and were used at the plantation in days gone by. In the old days every Creole house had its own *specialites,* of course, and they used to say — in fact everyone knew quite well — that if you asked a Creole lady for a recipe she would always omit a little something — just a little, you know — so that it would never turn out the same. Yes, friends would come to dine at *Belle Alliance,* shall we say, and all would speak of some delicious sauce or galantine or gumbo. How perfect! Someone would say, you must give me the recipe, and the hostess would say yes, indeed, with the greatest pleasure; but everyone knew that it would not be just right. Yes, that's the way it was.

"You know, Tante, what Celimene says?" puts in her nephew.

"My nephew means Celimene's saying to me, 'Madame,' she said, yes, "Madame, cookin' is a jalous business' I'm afraid 'tis so. Quite Jealous."

"I must tell you a story about that," W — says.

"Oh darling, *cher* darling, these stories!"

As he begins the story I find myself gazing at the portrait on the wall above the sofa. It is the same lady, but the years have passed; in the picture there are the young eyes, a little veiled, the profile like a goddess on a medal, and a pile of bright gold hair. You gather that Mrs. T — was not wooed solely for her recipes.

W — 's story is that one day he heard in his aunt's room a considerable argument going on between her and Celimene. It seemed that some time before, a year or two perhaps, she had given Celimene a recipe; and now after so long, when she tried to recall it, she could not exactly do so, and had to ask Celimene.

Celimene would not give it back to her.

* * *

Stark Young (1881 - 1963) was born in Como, Mississippi, where his father was a physician. He received a degree from the University of Mississippi in 1901 and then completed his Master's Degree at Columbia University in New York the following year. He taught at the University of Mississippi from 1905 to 1907; then he relocated to the University of Texas at Austin, where he established the *Texas Review*. In 1915 he moved to Amherst College in Massachusetts and taught English until 1921.

Subsequently, he moved to New York City and was named editor of *Theater Arts Magazine* for a while before becoming a drama critic for the *New Republic* and *the New York Times*. He published several novels, including his bestselling *So Red the Rose*, which dealt with the aftermath of the Civil War.

The book was adapted as a film that starred Margaret Sullivan. In his spare time, he translated plays by Anton Chekhov (*The Sea Gull* and the *Three Sisters*, are two examples) that were published by Modern Library. He was a leading intellectual of his generation.

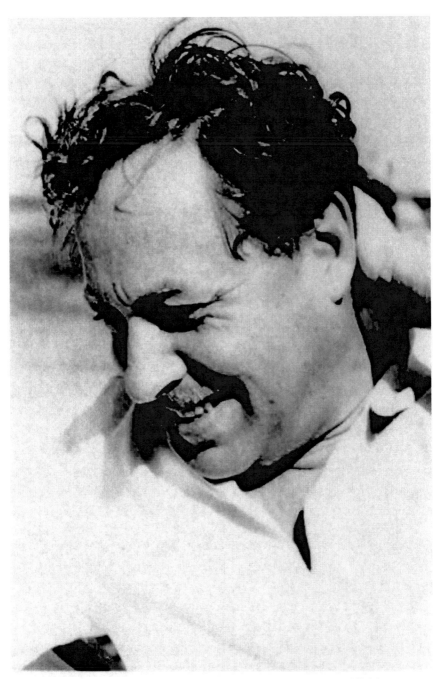

Tennessee Williams / Photo courtesy New Directions Publishing

MAMA'S OLD STUCCO HOUSE

BY TENNESSEE WILLIAMS

Mr. Jimmy Krenning wandered into the noon blaze of the kitchen for his breakfast coffee just wearing the shorts he had slept in. He's lost so much weight that summer that the shorts barely hung on his narrow hipbones and thin belly. At first the colored girl, Brinda, who had lately taken the place of her bed-ridden mother at the Krennings', had been offended as well as embarrassed by this way he had of walking around in front of her as if she were not a young girl and not even human, as if she were a dog in there waiting on him. She was a shy, pretty girl, brought up with more gentility than most white girls in the town of Macon, Georgia.

At first she thought he acted with this kind of impropriety around her because she was colored. That was when it offended her. Now she'd come to understand that Mr. Jimmy would have acted the same way with a white girl, with anybody of any race or any age or upbringing — he really and truly was so un-conscious of being with anybody when he entered the kitchen for his coffee that it was a wonder he smiled or spoke when he entered. It was Mr. Jimmy's nights that made him behave that way. They left him as dazed as a survivor of a plane crash in which everyone but Mr. Jimmy had died and now that she understood this, Brinda was no longer offended, but she was still embarrassed. She kept her eyes carefully away from him, but this was hard to do because he sat on the edge of the kitchen table, directly in the streak of noon blaze through the door, drinking coffee out of the Silex instead of the cup she'd put on the kitchen table.

She asked him if the coffee was hot enough for him. It had been off the stove since she heard him get out of bed half an hour ago. But Mr. Jimmy was so inattentive this morning he thought she was making a reference to the weather and said, God yes, this heat is breaking my balls.

This was the kind of talk that Brinda's mother had advised her to pretend not to hear. He don't mean nothing by it, her mother had explained to her. He's just acting smart or been drinking too much when he talks that way, and the best way to stop it is to pretend you don't hear it. When I get back to the Krennings', I'll straighten that boy out.

Brinda's Mama still expected, or pretended to expect, to return to work at the Krennings', but Brinda knew that her Mama was on her deathbed. It was a strange thing that Brinda's Mama and Mr. Jimmy's Mama had both took mortally sick the same summer, Mr. Jimmy's with a paralytic stroke and Brinda's with chronic liver trouble which had now reached a stage where she wasn't likely to ever get back on her feet. Even so, Brinda's Mama was better off than Mr. Jimmy's, who lay up there in that big old brass bed of hers absolutely speechless and motionless so that nobody knew if she was conscious or not, and had been like that since the first week of June which was three months ago. Although Brinda's Mama didn't know that it was the end for herself, she knew it was the end for old Mrs. Krenning and she sorrowed for her, asking Brinda each evening if Mrs.

Krenning had shown any sign of consciousness during the day. Sometimes there were little things to report, some days it seemed that Mrs. Krenning was more alive in her eyes than other days, and a few times she had seemed to be making an effort to speak. She had to be spoon-fed by Brinda or the nurse and some days she'd reject the spoon with her teeth and other days accept it and swallow about half what she given before beginning to let the soft food spill out her sunken gray jaw.

Brinda also cooked for Mr. Jimmy, she prepared his lunch and dinner, but he rarely would eat. She told her Mama it was a waste of food and time to cook for him, but her Mama said she had to keep on preparing the meals anyway and set the dinning-room table for him whether he came down to it or not when she rang the dinner bell for him. Now Brinda only made cold things, such as thin-sliced sandwiches which she could wrap in glazed paper and leave in the icebox for him.

The icebox was packed full of Mr. Jimmy's uneaten lunches and dinners, saucers and little bowls were stacked on top of each other, and the some mornings she would come in to find that during the night the big supply was suddenly cut down as if a gang of hungry guests had raided the icebox, and the kitchen table would be littered with remnants in dishes, and Brinda knew that that was exactly what had happened, that Mr. Jimmy had brought a crowd home the night before and they'd raided the icebox and devoured its store of meals for Mr. Jimmy that he had ignored.

But Brinda no longer told her Mama how things were going at the Krennings' because one day her Mama had struggled out of bed and come over to the house to make an effort to straighten out Mr. Jimmy. But when she got there she was too weak and breathless to talk. All she could do was look at him and shake her head and shed tears and she couldn't get up the stairs to see Mrs. Krenning, so Mr. Jimmy had to support her out to his car and drive her back home. In the car she panted like an old dog and was only able to say, Oh, Mr. Jimmy, why are you doing like this?

So this morning Brinda waited outside long enough for Mr. Jimmy to finish his breakfast coffee. Sometimes after his coffee he would come blinking and squinting out the back screen door and cross to his "studio," a little whitewashed building with a skylight, which no one but he ever entered. Its walls had no windows to peek in, but once when he drove into town he'd eft the door open, and Brinda went out to close it and saw inside a scene of terrible violence as if a storm, or a demon, had been caged in it, but now it was very quiet, only a fly buzzed in it, as if the storm or the demon that had smashed and turned every-thing over beneath the skylight's huge blue eye had fallen ex-hausted or died.

Brinda had considered going in to try to straighten it up, but there was something about the disorder, something unnat-ural about it that made it seem dangerous to enter, and so she just closed the door and returned to the comforting business of making up beds in the house. In the house there was always more than one bed to make up, not counting Mrs. Krenning's The old woman's bed was made up by her night nurse and the soiled sheets put in the hall for Brinda to wash. There had been five night nurses for Mrs. Krenning since Brinda had taken her Mama's place at the house, and each of them had left with the same complaint, that the nights in the house were too outra-geous to cope with. Now there was a male nurse talking care of the old lady at night, a repulsively coarse young man, red-headed, with arms as big as hams, covered with a fuzz of white hair. Brinda was too scandalized by this change to even speak of it to her Mama. She was afraid to go upstairs at the Kren-nings' until the day nurse came on at eleven. Once, when she had to go up to rouse Mr. Jimmy for a long-distance telephone call from New York, the male nurse had blocked her way on the back stairs, crouching, grinning and sticking his tongue out at her. She said, Excuse me, please, and tried to duck past him, and he had reached up after her and snatched her back down with one arm, like a red ham come to life, while the hand of the other made rough, breathtaking grabs at her breasts and belly, so that she screamed and screamed till Mr. Jimmy and his guest for the night ran naked out of his bedroom and the nurse had to let her go, pretending that he was just kidding. He called Mr. Jimmy "Cookie" and Mrs. Krenning "Old Faithful.," and filled the sickroom with candy-bar wrappings and empty pint bottles and books of colored comics, and ever since he had gone on duty at night Brinda felt she could see a look that was like an outcry of horror in the paralyzed woman's eyes when she would come up with her soft-boiled eggs in the mornings.

This morning it was the male nurse, not Jimmy, who stumbled out, blinking and squinting, onto the little porch off the kitchen. Hey, Snow White, he hollered, come in here, Cookie wants you!

Brinda had taken out some of Mrs. Krenning's washed bedclothes to dry in the yard and had deliberately stretched out, as long as she could, the process of hanging the heavy wet sheets on the clothesline to give the male nurse time to leave before she returned to the house, but he had hung around, this morning, a whole hour longer than usual when he came out to holler at her. Brinda returned to the kitchen to find that Mr. Jimmy was still sitting in there, although he had switched from coffee to whiskey and from the edge of the table to a kitchen chair.

Miss Brinda, he said, blinking and squinting at her as if at the noonday sun, that son-of-a-bitch night nurse says Mama's just gone ... Brinda began to cry, automatically but sincerely, standing before Mr. Jimmy. He took her hand gently in his, and then, to her shame and dismay, Brinda moved a step forward and took his bare white shoulders into her arms, enfolded them like a lost child's in her dark honey-colored bare arms, and his head dropped down to her shoulder, rested on it lightly for a moment, and to her still greater dismay, Miss Brinda felt her hand seize the close-cropped back of his head and pull it

70

tighter against her as if she wanted to bruise her shoulder with it. He let her do it for a moment or two, slaying nothing, making no motion, before he pushed her gently away by his two hands on her waist and said, Miss Brinda, you better go up and clean the room up a little before they come for Mama . . . .

Brinda waited at the foot of the back stairs till she was certain the male nurse wasn't up there, then she went up and entered old Mrs. Krenning's bedroom. One glance told her that the old lady was gone. She caught her breath and ran about the room making a quick collection of sticky candy-bar wrappings, pint bottles and chocolate-smeared comic books, the litter in which Mrs. Krenning had flown from the world, still speechless, unable to cry, and then Brinda ran back down to the kitchen. She found herself shouting orders at Mr. Jimmy.

Mr. Jimmy, go upstairs and take a cold shower and shave and put on some clean white clothes because your Mama has gone!

Mr. Jimmy grunted in a vague sort of agreement, drew a long breath and went back upstairs while Brinda phoned the white people's undertaker, whose name and number, at her mother's instruction, she had penciled on the back leaf of Mr. Jimmy's little black book of telephone numbers.

From the upstairs she could hear Mr. Jimmy's voice on the downstairs phone, speaking very low and unexcitedly to someone about what had happened, and presently the front doorbell started ringing and various young friends of Mr. Jimmy's began coming into the house, all seeming sober and talking in unusually quiet voices.

Brinda put on her simple, clean white hat and ran to her Mama's. She knew that her Mama would make another effort to get out of bed and come over, but it seemed justified, this time, by the occasion. She was right about it. Her Mama wept a little and then said, Help me get up, Brinda, I got to go over there and see that it's handled right.

This time she seemed much firmer, although the effort to

rise was probably even greater. Brinda got a cab for her. Holding her Mama's waist she could feel how thin the old dying woman had gotten, skin and bones now, but she walked with a slow steady stride to the cab and sat up very straight in it. Presently they arrived at the Krennings' big house of worn-out stucco, now full of the friends of Mr. Jimmy with only two or three older people who were, or had been at some time, close friends of old Mrs. Krenning's. The atmosphere in the house was appropriately subdued, shades drawn, and everyone looking politely sympathetic, not putting on a false show, but observing the conventional attitude toward a death. There were a good many young men from the local air base present, but they were being nice too, talking softly and acting with suitable decorum. They all had drinks in their hands, but they were all keeping sober, and when the undertaker's assistants carried old Mrs. Krenning downstairs and out of the house on a sheet-covered stretcher they kept a perfect silence except for one sobbing girl, who had risen abruptly and clutched Mr. Jimmy's shoulders, enjoying her burst of emotion.

Mr. Jimmy's glaze of detachment fell off him the very moment the door closed behind the men removing his mother from the house.

Okay, she's gone! And now I'm going to tell about my Mama! She was hard as my fist!

Oh, Jimmy, the sobbing girl pleaded. He pushed her away and struck his fist on a little chair-side table so hard that his drink bounced off it.

She was harder than my fist on this table! And she never let up on me once in my whole life, never! She was hard as my fist, she was harder than my goddamn fist on this table, and that's the truth about her. But now she's gone from this house and she's not going to come back to it, so the house is mine now. Well, she owned me, she used to own me, like she owned this house, and she was hard as my fist and she was tight as my fist, she set on her goddamn money like an old hen on a glass egg, she was tight and hard as my fist. I just got away once, that's all, just once in my life did I ever get away from her — an old faggot took me to New York with him and got tired of me there and told me to hit the street, and that's what I did, oh brother!

You want to know something? Even after I came back to this place, I never got a key to it, I never had my own door key. Not until after her stroke did I even have my own door key!

She'd lock up the house after supper, and if I'd gone out, she'd sit here waiting for me in this here chair. And you know what gave her the stroke? One night I came home and saw her through a front window sitting here waiting for me, to let me in when I rung the friggin' front doorbell, but I didn't ring it, I didn't knock or call, I just kicked the goddamn door in. I kicked it in and she let out with a cry like a pig being slaughtered. And when I entered, when I come in the kicked-open door, she was lyin' here paralyzed on tis here livin'-room floor, and never spoke or moved since, that was the way the old woman got her stroke. Well now, look here! Look at what I'm keepin' now in my pocket. See? Ev'ry goddamn key to Mama's old stucco house!

He took out of his pants pocket and raised up and jangled a big bunch of keys on a brass ring ornamented by a pair of red dice.

Then a soft voice stopped him my calling, Mr. Jimmy!

It was Brinda's Mama, in the shadowy next room. He nodded slightly, his outburst over as suddenly as it burst out. He threw the keys in the air and caught them and thrust them back in his pocket and sank back down in a chair, all in one movement it seemed, and just at that moment, luckily no sooner, the minister and his wife arrived at the door and the former decorum fell back over the parlor as if it had only lifted to the ceiling and hung up there until the outburst was over and then had settled back down again undamaged.

Brinda was amazed by the strength of her Mama. It seemed to come back like a miracle to the old woman. She set to work in the kitchen preparing a large platter of thin-cut sandwiches, boiled two Silexes of coffee and emptied them into the big silver percolator, and set the dining-room table as nicely as if for a party, knowing where everything was that would make the best show, the best linen and silver, the five-branched candelabra and even a set of finger bowls and lace napkins.

Mr. Jimmy stayed in the parlor, though, and drank his liquor till late in the afternoon, ignoring the buffet lunch that Brinda's Mama set for condolence callers. Only the minister and a few other old ladies drifted into the living room and ate a little bit of it. Then sundown came, the company dispersed and Mr. Jimmy went out. Brinda's Mama lay down on a cot in the basement, her hand on the side that pained her but her face, which was only slightly darker than Brinda's, looking composed and solemn. Brinda sat with her awhile and they talked in a desultory fashion as the light faded through the small high windows in the basement walls.

The talk had run out completely and the light was all but gone when Mr. Jimmy was heard coming back in the house. Brinda's Mama had seemed to be dozing but now her dark eyes opened and she cleared her throat and, turning her head to Brinda still seated beside her, directed her to ask Mr. Jimmy to come downstairs for a minute so she could talk to him before they went back home.

Brinda delivered this message to Mr. Jimmy who said, in reply, Bring your Mama upstairs and I'll drive you all back in the car.

Brinda's Mama's strength had all gone again and it was a struggle getting her up from the basement. She sat down, panting by the kitchen table while Mr.. Jimmy took a shower upstairs. Several times her head jerked forward and Brinda caught at her to hold her in the chair. But when Mr. Jimmy came down, she summoned her force back again and rose from the chair. They rode through the town in silence, to the section for Negroes, and not till Mr. Jimmy was about to pull up at their door did Brinda's Mama speak to him. Then she said:

Mr. Jimmy, what in the name of the Lord has happened to you? What kind of life are you leading here nowadays?

He answered her gently: Well, y'know, I did no good in New York ...

That's the truth, said Brinda's Mama, with sad conviction. You just got mixed with bad people and caught their bad ways ... And how come you give up your painting?

Brinda was scared when her Mama asked that question because, soon after she'd taken her Mama's place at the Krennings', she'd said to Mr. Jimmy one morning, when she was giving him coffee, Mr. Jimmy Mama keeps askin' me if you work on your studio after breakfast an' when I tell her you don't, it seems to upset her so much that now I tell her you do, but I hate to lie to Mama, 'cause I think she knows when I'm lyin' ...

That morning was the one time that Jimmy had been unkind to Brinda, not just unkind but violent. He had picked up a Silex of coffee and thrown it at the wall in the kitchen, and the kitchen wall was still brown-stained where the glass coffeepot had smashed on it. He had followed this action with a four-letter word, and then he had dropped his head in his shaking hands.

So Brinda expected something awful to happen at this moment in response to her Mama's bold question, but all Mr. Jimmy did was to drive right through a red light at a street intersection.

Brinda's Mama said, You went through a stoplight, and Mr. Jimmy answered, Did I? Well, that's O.K. ....

It was a fair distance from the Krennings' house to Brinda's and her Mama's, and a few blocks after Mr. Jimmy had driven through the stoplight, Mr. Jimmy slowed the car down again and the talk was continued.

Mr. Jimmy said, If I don't know, who knows?

Well, said Brinda's Mama, even if you quit workin' you

can't do nothin', just nothin', you got to do somethin', don't you?

I do something, said Mr. Jimmy.

What do you do?

Well, about this time of evening, I drive out by the air base, I go a little bit past it, and then I turn around and drive back, and, here and there, along the road back into town, I pass young fliers thumbing a ride into town, and I pick out one to pick up, and I pick him up and we go to the house and we drink and discuss ourselves with each other and drink and, after a while, well, maybe we get to be friends or maybe we don't, and that's what I do now, you . . .

He slowed the car down toward the house, stopped it right in front of the walk to the porch, with a deep sighing intake of breath, and released the wheel and his head fell back as if his neck was broken.

Brinda's Mama sighed too, and her head now only fell back against the car cushion but lolled to the side a little. They were like two broken-necked people, and with the uncomprehending patience of a dog, Brinda just sat and waited for them both to revive.

Then, at last, Mr. Jimmy sighed again, with a long intake of breath, and lurched out of the car and came around to the back seat to open the door for them as if they were two white ladies.

He not only assisted Brinda's Mama out of the car, but he kept a tight hold on her up to the porch. Perhaps if he hadn't she would have fallen down, but Brinda could sense that it was something more than one person giving another a necessary physical support for a little distance, and when they had got up the front steps, Mr. Jimmy still stayed. He took in his breath very loudly again with the same sighing sound as he had done twice before, and there was a prolonged hesitation, which Brinda found awkward and tense, though it did not seem to bother either her Mama or Mr. Jimmy. It was like something they were used to, or had always expected. They stood there at the top of the steps to the porch, and it was uncertain whether they were going to part at this point or going to remain together for a while longer.

They seemed like a pair of people who quarreled and come to an understanding, not because of any agreement between them, but because of a mutual recognition of a sad, inescapable thing that gave them a closeness even through disappointment in trying to settle their quarrel.

Brinda's Mama said, Mr. Jimmy, sit down with us a little, and he did.

Both of the two chairs on the front porch were rockers. Brinda sat on the steps, Mr. Jimmy rocked, but her Mama sat still in her chair.

After a little while Brinda's Mama said, Mr. Jimmy, what are you going to do now?

I make no plans, I just go along, go along.

How long you plan to do that?

Long as I can, till something stops me, I guess.

Brinda's Mama nodded and then was silent as if inwardly calculating the length of time that might take. The silence continued as long as it might have taken her to arrive at a conclusion to this problem, and then she got up and said I am going to die now, as quietly as if she had only said she was going in the dark house. Mr. Jimmy stood up as if a white lady had risen and held the screen door open while she unlocked the wooden one.

Brinda started in after her, but her Mama blocked her way in.

You go stay at the Krennings', you go on back there tonight an' clean up that mess in the place and you two stay there together and you look after each other, and, Brinda, don't let them white boys interfere with you. When you hear them come in, go down to the basement and lock the basement door an' you stay down there till daylight, unless Mr. Jimmy calls for you, and if he calls for you, go up an' see what he wants.

Then she turned to Mr. Jimmy and said, I thought a white boy like you was born with a chance in the world!

She then shut the door and locked it. Brinda couldn't believe that her Mama had locked her out, but that's what she'd done. She would have stayed there senselessly waiting before that locked door, but Mr. Jimmy gently took hold of her arm and led her out to his car. He opened the back door for her as if she were a white lady. She got in the car and going home, to the Krennings', Mr. Jimmy serenely drove through the stoplights as if he were color-blind. He drove home straight and fast and when they arrived at the Krennings' Brinda observed that a soft light seemed to say something that no one had said all day in so many words, that God, like other people, has two kinds of hands, one hand with which to strike and another to soothe and caress with.

* * *

Thomas Lanier "Tennessee" Williams (1911 – 1983) was born in the parsonage of St. Paul's Episcopal Church in Columbus, Mississippi, and subsequently lived in Clarksdale, Mississippi, located in the heart of the Mississippi Delta, before the family moved to St. Louis, Missouri. His alcoholic father was a traveling salesman and spent a great deal of time away from home. His sister Rose was diagnosed with schizophrenia as a young woman and underwent a lobotomy with disastrous results that required her to be institutionalized for the rest of her life. Once he reached a point in life that he could do so he moved her to a private facility just outside New York City. He visited her often and gave her a percentage interest in several of his successful plays so that she could continue to be cared for at the institution.

After finishing college, Williams moved to New Orleans, where he lived for many years. He was a playwright, novelist, and short story writer. By 1959, he had earned two Pulitzer Prizes, and a Tony Award. Because of plays such as *A Streetcar Named Desire, Cat on a Hot Tin Roof, the Glass Menagerie, Suddenly Last Summer,* and *The Night of the Iguana,* his is today considered one of the most important playwrights of the 20th Century. In 1979, he was inducted into the American Theater Hall of Fame.

THE BOY IN THE TREE

BY ELIZABETH SPENCER

On a February afternoon, Wallace Harkins is driving out of town on a five-mile country road to see his mother. He was born and raised in the house where she lives, but the total impracticality of keeping an aging lady out there alone in that large a place is beginning to trouble him.

His mother does not know he is coming. He used to try to telephone, but sometimes she doesn't answer. She will never admit either to not hearing the ring, or to not being in the mood to pick up the receiver, though one or the other must be true.

At the moment Mrs. Harkins is polishing some silver at the kitchen sink. At times she looks out in the yard. In winter the pecan trees are gray and bare — a network of gray branches, the ones near the trunk large as a man's wrist, the smaller ones reaching out, lacing and dividing, all going toward cold outer air. Sometimes Mrs. Harkins sees a boy sitting halfway up a tree, among the branches. Who is he? Why is he there? Sometimes he isn't there.

She often looks out the back rather than the front. For one

thing the kitchen is in the back of the house, so it's easy. But for another, there is expectation. Of What? That she doesn't know. Of someone? Of something? Strange mule, strange dog, strange man or woman? So far lately there has only been the boy. When her son Wallace appears out of nowhere (she hasn't heard the car), she tells him about it.

"Sure you're not seeing things?" he teases.

"I do see things," she tells him, "but the things I see are there."

He hopes she'll start seeing things that aren't there in order to talk her into a "retirement community."

"You mean a nursing home," she always says. "Call it what you mean."

"It isn't like that," he would counter.

"There isn't one here," she would object.

"Certainly there is. Just outside town. Two in fact, one out the other way."

"If I was there I wouldn't be here."

That was for sure. Once, over another matter, she had chased him out of the house waving the broom at him. She was laughing, to show she didn't really mean it, but then she dropped the broom and threw an old cracked teacup, which caught him back of the right ear and bled. "Oh, I'm so sorry," she said. And ran right up and kissed where it bled. But she was laughing still, the whole time. How did you know which she meant, the throwing or the kissing?

He dared to mention it to his wife Jenny when he got home. His mother and his wife had been at odds for so many years he believed they never thought of it anymore, but when he said, "Which did she mean?" his wife said immediately, "She doesn't know herself."

"You think she's gone around the bend?" he asked, and thought once again of the retirement home.

"I think she never was anywhere else," Jenny answered,

solving nothing. She was cleaning off the cut and dabbing on antiseptic which stung.

His problem was women, he told himself. But going up to his office that morning, he almost had a wreck.

The occasion was the sight of a boy standing on a street corner. It was the division of crossing streets just after passing the main business street and just before the block containing the post office and bank. The boy was wearing knee britches, completely out of date now, but just what he himself used to wear to school. They buttoned at the knee, only he had always found the buttons a nuisance, the wool cloth scratchy, and had unbuttoned them as soon as he got out of sight of his mother. As if that was not enough, the boy was eating peanuts! So what? He thought, but he knew the answer very well.

He himself had stood right there, many the day, and shelled a handful of peanuts, raw from the country, dirt still sticking to their shells. He always threw the shells out in the street. At that very moment, he saw the boy throw the shells the same way. Wallace almost ran into an oncoming car.

Once at the office, he was annoyed to find a litter of mail on his desk. Miss Carlton had not opened the envelopes and he was about to ring for her when she entered on her own, looking frazzled. "They all came back last night," she said. "I stayed up till two o'clock getting them something to eat and listening to all the stories. You'd think deer season was the only time worth living for. "

"Kill anything?" he asked, more automatically than not. He'd never been the hunting-fishing type.

"Oh, sure. One ten-pointer."

Was that good or bad? He sat slitting envelopes and had no reaction, one way or the other. He had once owned a dog, but animals in general didn't mean a lot to him.

The peanuts had been brought to him in from the country almost every day by a little white-headed girl who sat right in front of him in study hall. Once he'd found her after school, waiting for a ride (they both had missed the bus), and they went in the empty gym and tried making up how you kissed.

Had she missed the bus on purpose, knowing he'd be late from helping the principal clean up the chemistry lab? How did she ever get home? He never found out for it was not so long after that he had been taken sick.

They took him home from school with high fever. Several people put him to bed. It lasted a long time. His mother was always there. Whenever he woke up from a feverish sleep, there she'd be, right before him in her little rocking chair, reading or sewing. "Water," he would say, and she would give him some. "Orange juice," he said, and there it would be too.

He told his wife later, "I can't figure out how you can be sick and happy too. But I was. She was great to me."

"You like to be loved," his wife said, and gave him a hug.

"Doesn't everybody?"

"More or less."

When he went back to school the white-headed girl had left. Died or moved away? Now when he thought of her, he couldn't remember.

* * *

Wallace Harkins was assured of being a contented man, by and large. When troubles came, even small ones looked bigger than they would to anyone with large ones. Yet he often puzzled over things and when he puzzled too long he would go out to see his mother and get more puzzled than ever. As for his state of bliss when he was sick as a boy and dependent on her devotion, he would wonder now if happiness always came in packages, wrapped up in time. Try to extend the time, and the package got stubborn. Not wanting to be opened, it just sat and remained the same. You couldn't get back in it because time had carried you on elsewhere.

It was the same with everything, wasn't it? There was that honeymoon time (though several years after they married, it had seemed like honeymoon) when he and Jenny got stranded in Jamaica because of a hurricane, no transport to the airport, no airport open. Great alarm at the resort hotel up the coast from Montego Bay, fears of being levelled and washed away. They ate by candlelight, and walked clinging to one another by a turbulent sea. "Let's just stay here," was Jenny's plea, and he had shared it. Oh Lord, he really did. But then it was over. When he thought of it, wind whistled around his ears, and out in the water a stricken boat bobbed desperately. They both had loved it and tried going back, but this time the food was dreary, the rates had gone up, and the sea was full of jellyfish.

* * *

"Mother," he asked her, "why do people change?"

She was looking out the back window. "Change from what?"

He'd no answer.

"How is Edith?" she asked. Edith was his daughter.

"Edie is failing Agnes Scott," he said. "She isn't dumb, she just doesn't apply herself."

"Then take her out for a while. Start all over."

I'll do that, he thought Time marched along. He had gray in his hair.

"Do you remember Amy Louise?" he asked, for the name of the white-haired girl had suddenly returned to him.

"That girl that came here and ate up a lot of candy once? It was when you were sick. I thought she'd never seen any candy before. Before she left, she had chocolate running out of her mouth."

"Did she have white hair?"

"No, just brown. You must mean somebody else."

He noted the street corner carefully when he drove home. Nobody was on it.

* * *

Wallace had always loved his wife Jenny from afar. When they were in high school together she hadn't the time of day for him, and the biggest of life's surprises came when years later she consented to marry him. "She's just on the rebound," said an unkind friend, for, as they both knew, she had been dating an ex-football player from State College, while working in Atlanta. "Just the same," said Wallace, "she said she would."

Jenny liked any number of things — being back in the town, a nice place to live, furniture to her taste, cooking and going on trips. She was easy to please. She even liked him in bed. Surprise? It was true that his desires were many, but realizations few. He had put himself down as a possible failure. With Jenny, all changed. She didn't object when for a warm-up he fondled her toes. She said it was better than tickling her. Who had tickled her? He didn't ask.

Jenny was pretty too. Shiny brown hair and clear smooth skin. He loved the bouncy way she walked and the things she laughed at. He told his mother that. She said that was good. But when anybody in their right mind would have to agree, thought Wallace. He caught himself thinking that. Was his mother not in her right mind? A puzzle.

"She makes you feel guilty," Jenny pointed out. "If I were you, I'd quit going out there so much. She's happy the way she is. If you didn't come, she wouldn't care."

"Really?" said Wallace. The thought pierced him, but he decided to try it.

* * *

About this time, Wallace had a strange dream. Like all his dreams, it had a literal source. Out in Galveston, Texas, a man had acquired a tiger club, a playful little creature. It grew up.

One summer day, responding to complaints from the neighbors, the animal control team found a great clumsy orange-colored beast chained in the backyard of an abandoned house. The chain was no more than three or four feet long and was fastened to an iron stake sunken in concrete. In fact, the only surface available to the animal was cement, the yard having been paved for parking. The sun was hot. The tiger at this stage resembled nothing so much as a rug not even the Salvation Army would take.

Reading about it, Jenny was riveted to the paper. "Where's the bastard took that cat in the first place?"

"They'll track him down."

"I hope they shoot him," she said.

"You don't mean the tiger?" Wallace teased her. She said she certainly didn't.

What do you do with a tiger?

The event made headlines locally because a preserve for large cats was located near their town. A popular talk show host agreed to the tiger's expenses for transportation, release, rehabilitation, psychiatric counseling, and nourishment.

"Good God," said Wallace, "they're going to have to slaughter a whole herd of cattle every weekend."

"Maybe it will like soybean hamburgers," said Jenny.

"Wonder if they ever found that guy."

"I've just been wondering if maybe the tiger ate him."

In his dream, some weeks later, Wallace looked out the back door window and saw the tiger, thoroughly cured and healthy, wandering around in the backyard. He went out to speak with it. He thought he was being courageous, as it might attack. At first it glanced up at him, gave a rumble of a growl, and wandered away as though bored. "You bastard," said Wallace. "Don't you appreciate anything?" Then he woke up.

* * *

The definitive quarrel between Jenny and Mrs. Harkins had taken place rather soon after Wallace's marriage. They were in the habit of going out to see the lady on Sunday afternoons and staying for what she called "a bite to eat." Sometimes she made up pancakes from Bisquick mix. Jenny was holding an electric hand beater and humming away on the batter when the machine slipped out of her hand and went leaping around first on the table, where it overturned the bowl with batter, then bounced off to the floor.

Jenny shouted, "I can't find the fucking switch!"

The beater went bounding around the room. She was trying to catch up with it, but found it hard to grab. Batter, meantime, soared around in splatters. Some of it hit the walls, some the ceiling, and some went in their faces and on their clothes. Mrs. Harkins jerked the plug out of its socket. Everything went still. Jenny licked batter off her mouth and grabbed a paper towel to mop Wallace's shirt. A blob had gone in Mrs. Harkins' hair. Jenny got laughing and couldn't stop, It seemed a weird accident. "I guess the shit hit the fan," she said.

Mrs. Harkins walked to the center of the room. "Anybody who uses your kind of language has got no right to be here."

"Mother!" said Wallace, turning white.

"Gosh," said Jenny, turning red. She walked out of the kitchen. There fell a silence Wallace thought would never end. He expected Jenny back, but then he heard the car pull out of the drive and speed away.

Mrs. Harkins set about cleaning pancake batter off everything in sight, and scrambled some eggs for their supper.

"I think you both ought to apologize," Wallace ventured, when his mother drove him home.

"You do?" said Mrs. Harkins, rather vaguely, as though unsure of what he was talking about.

"I never heard her say words like that before," Wallace vowed, though in truth Jenny did have a colorful vocabulary, restrained about Edith. In the long run, nobody apologized. But Jenny wouldn't go back with Wallace anymore. What she saw in her mother-in-law's announcement was that she (Jenny) was a lower-class woman, common, practically a redneck. "She didn't mean that," said Wallace.

"You can't tell me," said Jenny. Furthermore, she thought the results were exactly what Mrs. Harkins wanted. She didn't want to see Jenny. She had been waiting all along for something to happen.

Within himself, Wallace lamented the rift. But he finally came to consider that Jenny might be right. He took to going home to see about his mother. Gradually, this change of habit got to be the way things were. In routine lies contentment.

* * *

After the tiger dream Wallace went back again. He didn't know why, but felt he had to.

She wasn't there. The house still quiet and empty, she had even remembered to lock the door. The car was gone. He scribbled a note asking her to call him and went away reluctantly. She could be anywhere.

Wallace returned home but heard nothing. He fretted.

"Well," said his mother the next day (she hadn't called). "It was just that boy up in the tree. I finally went out and hollered up to ask him who he was and what he wanted. Then he came down. He just said he liked being around this house, and he wanted me to notice him. He was scared to knock and ask. He rambles. He's one of those rambling kind. Always wandering around in the woods. I drove him home. The family is just ordinary, but he seems a better sort. Smart." She tapped her head significantly.

"I dreamed about a tiger," said Wallace.

"What was he doing?" his mother asked.

"Prowling around in the backyard. It's that one they brought here from Texas."

"Maybe it got out," she suggested.

If only I could stick to business, thought Wallace.

* * *

That weekend Edith came home from Agnes Scott. She had flunked out of math courses, so could not fulfill her ambition to take a science major, a springboard into many fabulous careers, but had enrolled instead in communications. She had a boyfriend with her, a nice well-mannered intelligent boy named Phillip Barnes, who in about thirty minutes of his arrival had made up for Edie's inability to pass trigonometry. He knew how to listen to older people in an attentive way. He let it drop that his father ran a well-known horticultural company in Pennsylvania, but his mother being Southern had wanted him at Emory. He was working on his accent with Edie's help, he claimed, and did imitations to make them laugh, which they gladly did. He was even handsome.

Wallace, feeling proud, suggested they all go out to see Grandmother. Edith exchanged glances with her mother. "She won't know whether we come or not. Anyway, the house is falling down."

"She remembers what she wants to," said Wallace.

"He's got an Oedipus complex," said Jenny.

They argued for a while about such a visit but in the end Wallace, Edith and Phillip drove out on the excuse that the house, at least, was interesting being old.

On return they announced that Mrs. Harkins had not said very much, she just sat and looked at them. "Not unusual," said Jenny.

Wallace sighed with relief. For, as a matter of fact, the little his mother had said had been way too much. She appraised the two for some time, sitting with them in the wide hallway, drafty in winter, but cool in spring and summer, and remarked that a bird had flown in there this morning and didn't want to leave. "I chased him out with the broom," she said. Wallace well remembered that broom and wondered if she had made it up about the bird. Mrs. Harkins closed her eyes and appeared to be either thinking things over or dozing. Phillip Barnes conversed nicely on with Wallace.

Mrs. Harkins suddenly woke up. "If you two want to get married," she said, "you are welcome to do it here."

They all three burst out laughing and Edith said, "Really, Grandmamma, we haven't got halfway to that yet."

"You might," said Mrs. Harkins, and closed her eyes again.

"It really is a fine old house," said Phillip, who appreciated the upper-class look of old Southern homes.

Going out to the car, Wallace whispered to Edith not to mention what his mother had said. "You know they don't get on," he said.

But Phillip unfortunately had not heard him. Once back home, he laughed about it. "Edie's going to come downstairs in a hoop skirt," he laughed. But seriously, to Wallace, he said: "Gosh, I do like your mother. She pretends not to be listening, but I bet she hears everything. And what a great old house that is Thanks for taking us."

"What's this about a hoop skirt?" Jenny asked.

"Oh, nothing," said Edie.

But Phillip wouldn't stop. It seemed that Phillip didn't ever stop. "She said Edie could get married out there. Can't you just see her, carrying her little bouquet. Bet the lady's got it all planned."

* * *

No sooner were Edie and Phillip on the road to Atlanta than Jenny threw a fit. "What does that old woman mean?" she demanded. "She's doing what she always does. She's taking over what belongs to me!"

"But honey," Wallace said, "we don't even know they're apt to get married."

"They're in love, aren't they? Anything can happen. And don't you honey me."

"But sweetheart, maybe Mother meant well. Maybe she

saw an opportunity to get us all back together again."

"With her calling the shots. She's a meddlesome old bitch is what she is."

That was too much. Wallace had looked forward to an evening with Jenny, going over the whole visit a piece at a time, and afterwards having a loving time in bed. He wasn't to have anything of the sort tonight, he realized, and furthermore his mother was not a bitch.

"My mother is not a bitch," he said, and left the house.

How was he to know that Jenny had been mentally planning Edie's wedding herself? She had got as far as the bridesmaids' dresses, and was weighing black and white chiffon against a medley of various colors, not having got to what the mother-of-the-bride should appear in.

Wallace wandered. He drove around in the night. He thought of the tiger, but it was too late to look for the animal preserve. He thought of his mother, but he dreaded her seeing what was wrong. He'd no one to admit things to.

He went to a movie and felt sorry for himself. On the way out he saw a head of white-blonde hair going toward the exit. He hastened but there was only an older woman in those tight slacks Jenny disliked, wearing too much lipstick. He did not ask if her name was Amy Louise.

* * *

In spring Wallace threw himself madly into his work. He journeyed to Atlanta to an insurance salesman's conference, he plied his skills among local homeowners, car owners, small business owners. He even circulated in a trailer park and came out with a hefty list of new policies. What is it that you can't insure? Practically nothing.

Then, to his surprise, the way opened up for Wallace to make a lot of money. He received a call from some leading businessmen who wanted to talk something over. A small parcel of wooded land his father had left him just beyond the highway turnoff to the town was the object of their inquiry. Why didn't he develop it? Well, Wallace explained, he'd never thought about it. The truth was, in addition, he connected the land with his father who had died when Wallace was eleven and whom he did not clearly remember.

The little seventy-five or so acres was not pretty; it ran to irregular slopes and the scrappy growth of oaks and sycamore could scarcely be walked among for all the undergrowth. Still, Wallace paid the taxes every year, and thought of its very shaggy, natural appearance with a kind of affection, a leftover memory of his father, who had wanted him to have something of his very own. And he did go and walk around there, and though he came out scratched with briers, it made him feel good for some reason.

"Honey, we're going to be rich," Wallace said to Jenny.

"Why else you think I married you?" Jenny giggled, perking up.

Still what surprised him was his popularity. Prominent men squeezed his hand, they slapped his shoulder, they inquired after his mother, they recalled his father.

"Why do they like me?" he inquired of Jenny.

"Why not?" was Jenny's answer.

But he thought what it all had to do with business. And he was still puzzling besides over what had happened at the last business meeting. For they had succeeded with him; he was well along the road. Subdivision, surveys, sewage, drainage, electric power . . . But suddenly he had cried out:

"To hell with it! I don't want to!"

He sat frozen, wondering at himself, and looking about at the men in the room They had kept on talking, never missing a syllable. On leaving, he had asked one of the oldest, "Did I say anything funny?"

"Funny? Why no."

"I mean, didn't I yell something out?"

"Nothing I heard."

So he'd only thought it?

Standing in the kitchen that night, Wallace came across the real question in his life. He scratched his head and thought about it. "You and Edie, do you love me?"

"You like to be loved," Jenny said, and patted his stomach (he was getting fat). She stroked his head (he was getting bald).

She had calmed down since her explosion, but they both still remembered it and did not speak of it.

* * *

The trees were in full leaf when he next drove out to see Mrs. Harkins.

The front door was open but no one seemed to be downstairs. He stood in the hallway and wondered whether to call. From above he heard the murmur of voices, and so climbed up to see.

His mother was standing in one of the spare rooms. With her was a boy, maybe about fifteen. A couple of old leather suitcases lay open on the bed, the contents partially pulled out and scattered over the coverlet. She was holding up to the boy a checkered shirt which Wallace remembered well, a high school favorite.

"Isn't it funny? I never thought to give away all these clothes?" she said.

The boy was standing obediently before her. When she held up the shirt he drew the sleeve along one arm to check the length. He was a dark boy, nearly grown, with black hair topping a narrow intelligent face set with observant eyes. Truth was he did measure out a bit like Wallace at a young age, though Wallace had reddish brown hair and large coppery freckles. They stared at each other and thought of nothing to say.

"This is Martin Grimsley," said Mrs. Harkins. "Martin, this is my son Wallace."

"The boy in the tree?" Wallace asked.

"The same," said Mrs. Harkins, and held up a pair of trousers which buttoned at the knee. "Plus fours," she said.
"Too hot for now, but maybe this winter."

She had made some chicken salad for lunch with an aspic, iced tea and biscuits and banana pudding. Wallace stayed to eat.

"Wallace saw the tiger," said Mrs. Harkins.

The boy brightened. "They keep him out near us with all them others."

"All those others," said Mrs. Harkins.

"I can hear 'em growling and coughing at night."

Wallace asked: "Did you stand on a corner uptown eating peanuts?"

"Not that I know of," responded Martin Grimsley.

They lingered there on the porch while the day waned.

Martin Grimsley talked. He talked on and on. He had been up Holders Creek to where it started. He had seen a nest of copperheads. Once he had seen a rattlesnake, but it had spots, so maybe it wasn't. He liked the swamps, but he especially liked the woods, different ones.

Inside the telephone rang. Nobody moved to answer it. They sat there listening to Martin Grimsley, until the lightning bugs began to wink, out beyond the drive.

"Someday we'll go and see," said Mrs. Harkins.

"See what?" said Wallace.

"The tiger," said the boy. "She means the tiger."

"Of course," said Mrs. Harkins.

They kept on talking about the countryside. Wallace wandered with them, listening. He watched the line of the

woods where the property ended. There the girl with silver hair would appear, the tiger walking beside her.

He was happy and he did not see why not.

* * *

Elizabeth Spencer (1921 -   ) was born in Carrollton Mississippi, not far from Greenwood. After obtaining degrees at Belhaven College in Jackson and Vanderbilt University in Nashville, she worked as a reporter at the Nashville Tennessean for a while and then accepted a teaching position at the University of Mississippi. Before moving to Chapel Hill, North Carolina, where she lives today, she lived in Italy and Montreal, Canada. To date she has written nine novels, including *The Voice at the Back Door* and *The Light in the Piazza*, which was made into a movie in 1962, and eight short story collections.

Richard Wright / The Library of Congress

BIG BLACK GOOD MAN

BY RICHARD WRIGHT

Through the open window Olaf Jenson could smell the sea and hear the occasional foghorn of a freighter; outside, rain pelted down through an August night, drumming softly upon the pavements of Copenhagen, inducing drowsiness, bringing dreamy memory, relaxing the tired muscles of his work-wracked body. He sat slumped in a swivel chair with his legs outstretched and his feet propped atop an edge of his desk. An inch of white ash tipped the end of his brown cigar and now and then he inserted the end of the stogie into his mouth and drew gently upon it, letting wisps of blue smoke eddy from the corners of his wide, thin lips.

The watery gray irises behind the thick lenses of his eye-glasses gave him a look of abstraction, of absent-mindedness, of an almost genial idiocy. He sighed, reached for his half-empty bottle of beer, and drained it into his glass and downed

it with a long slow gulp, then licked his lips replacing the cigar, he slapped his right palm against his thigh
and said half aloud:

"Well, I'll be sixty tomorrow. I'm not rich but I'm not poor either ... Really, I can't complain. Got good health. Traveled all over the world and had my share of the girls when I was young ... And my Karen's a good wife. I own my home. Got no debts. And I love digging in my garden in the spring ... Grew the biggest carrots of anybody last year. Ain't saved much money, but what the hell ... Money ain't everything. Got a good job. Night portering ain't too bad."

He shook his head and yawned.

"Karen and I could have had some children, though. Would have been good company ... 'Specially for Karen. And I could of taught 'em languages ... English, French, German, Danish, Swedish, Norwegian, and Spanish ... "

He took the cigar out of his mouth and eyed the white ash critically.

"Hell of a lot of good language learning did me ... Never got anything out of it But those ten years in New York were fun ... Maybe I could of got rich if I'd stayed in America ... Maybe. But I'm satisfied. You can't have everything."

Behind him the office door opened and a young man, a medical student occupying room number nine, entered.

"Good evening," the student said.

"Good evening," Olaf said, turning.

The student went to the keyboard and took hold of the round, brown knob that anchored his key.

"Rain, rain, rain," the student said.

"That's Denmark for you," Olaf smiled at him.

"This dampness keeps me clogged up like a drainpipe," the student complained.

"That's Denmark for you," Olaf repeated with a smile.

"Good night," the student said.

"Good night, son," Olaf sighed, watching the door close.

Well, my tenants are my children, Olaf told himself. Almost all of his children were in their rooms now . . . Only seventy-two and forty-four were missing . . . Seventy-two might've gone to Sweden . . . And forty-four was maybe staying at his girl's place tonight, like he sometimes did . . . He studied the pear-shaped blobs of hard rubber, reddish brown like ripe fruit, that hung from the keyboard, then glanced at his watch.

Only room thirty, eighty-one, and one hundred and one were empty . . . And it was almost midnight. In a few moments he could take a nap. Nobody hardly ever came looking for accommodations after midnight, unless a stray freighter came in, bringing thirsty, women-hungry sailors. Olaf chuckled softly. Why in the hell was I ever a sailor? The whole time I was at sea I was thinking and dreaming about women. Then why didn't I stay on land where women could be had? Hunh? Sailors are crazy . . .

But he liked sailors. They reminded him of his youth, and there was something so direct, simple, and childlike about them. They always said straight out what they wanted, and what they wanted was almost always women and whisky . . . "Well, there's no harm in that . . . Nothing could be more natural," Olaf sighed, looking thirstily at his empty beer bottle. No; he'd not drink any more tonight; he'd had enough; he'd go to sleep . . .

He was bending forward and loosening his shoelaces when he heard the office door crack open. He lifted his eyes, then sucked in his breath. He did not straighten; he just stared up and around at the huge black thing that filled the doorway. His reflexes refused to function; it was not fear; it was just simple astonishment. He was staring at the biggest, strangest, and blackest man he'd ever seen in all his life.

"Good evening," the black giant said in a voice that filled the small office. "Say, you got a room?"

Olaf sat up slowly, not to answer but to look at this brood

ing black vision; it towered darkly some six and a half feet into the air, almost touching the ceiling; and its skin was so black that it had a bluish tint. And the sheer bulk of the man! . . . His chest bulged like a barrel; his rocklike and humped shoulders hinted of mountain ridges; the stomach ballooned like a threatening stone; and the legs were like telephone poles . . . The big black cloud of a man now lumbered into the office, bending to get its buffalolike head under the door frame, then advanced slowly upon Olaf, like a stormy sky descending.

"You got a room? The big black man asked again in a resounding voice.

Olaf now noticed that the ebony giant was well dressed, carried a wonderful new suitcase, and wore black shoes that gleamed despite the raindrops that peppered their toes.

"You're American?" Olaf asked him.

"Yeah, man; sure," the black giant answered.

"Sailor?"

"Yeah. American Continental Lines."

Olaf had not answered the black man's question. It was not that the hotel did not admit men of color; Olaf took in all comers — blacks, yellows, whites, and browns . . . To Olaf, men were men, and, in his day, he'd worked and eaten and slept and fought with all kinds of men. But this particular black man . . . Well, he didn't seem human. Too big, too black, too loud, too direct, and probably too violent to boot . . . Olaf's five feet seven inches scarcely reached the black giant's shoulder and his frail body weighed less, perhaps, than one of the man's gigantic legs . . . There was something about the man's intense blackness and ungamely bigness that frightened and insulted Olaf; he felt as though this man had come here expressly to remind him how puny, how tiny, and how weak and how white he was. Olaf knew, while registering his reactions, that he was being irrational and foolish; yet, for the first time in his life, he was emotionally determined to refuse a man a room solely on the basis of the man's size and color . . .

Olaf's lips parted as he groped for the right words in which to couch his refusal, but the black giant bent forward and boomed:

"I asked you if you got a room. I got to put up somewhere tonight, man."

"Yes, we got a room," Olaf murmured.

And at once he was ashamed and confused. Sheer fear had made him yield. And he seethed against himself for is involuntary weakness. Well he'd look over his book and pretend that he'd made a mistake; he'd tell this hunk of blackness that there was really no free room in the hotel, and that he was so sorry . . . Then, just as he took out the hotel register to make believe that he was poring over it, a thick roll of American bank notes, crisp and green, was thrust under his nose.

"Keep this for me, will you?" the black giant commanded. "Cause I'm gonna get drunk tonight and I don't wanna lose it."

Olaf stared at the roll; it was huge, in denominations of fifties and hundreds. Olaf's eyes widened.

"How much is there?" he asked.

"Two thousand six hundred," the giant said. "Just put it into an envelope and write 'Jim' on it and lock it in your safe, hunh?"

The black mass of man had spoken in a manner that indicated that it was taking it for granted that Olaf would obey. Olaf was licked. Resentment clogged the pores of his wrinkled white skin. His hands trembled as he picked up the money. No; he couldn't refuse this man . . . The impulse to deny him was strong, but each time he was about to act upon it something thwarted him, made him shy off. He clutched about desperately for an idea. Oh, yes, he could say that if he planned to stay for only one night, then could not have the room, for it was against the policy of the hotel to rent rooms for only one night . . "

"How long are you staying? Just tonight?" Olaf asked.

"Naw I'll be here for five or six days, I reckon," the giant answered offhandedly.

"You take room number thirty," Olaf heard himself saying. "It's forty kronor a day."

"That's all right with me," the giant said.

With slow, stiff movements, Olaf put the money in the safe and then turned and stared helplessly up into the living breathing blackness looming above him. Suddenly he became conscious of the outstretched palm of the black giant; he was silently demanding the key to the room. His eyes downcast, Olaf surrendered the key, marveling at the black man's tremendous hands . . . He could kill me with one blow, Olaf told himself in fear.

Feeling himself beaten, Olaf reached for the suitcase, but the black hand of the giant whisked it out of his grasp.

"That's too heavy for you, big boy; I'll take it," the giant said.

Olaf let him. He thinks I'm nothing . . . He led the way down the corridor, sensing the giant's lumbering presence behind him. Olaf opened the door of number thirty and stood politely to one side, allowing the black giant to enter. At once the room seemed like a doll's house, so dwarfed and filled and tiny it was with a great living blackness . . . Flinging his suitcase upon a chair, the giant turned. The two men looked directly at each other now.

Olaf saw that the giant's eyes were tiny and red, buried, it seemed, in muscle and fat. Black cheeks spread, flat and broad, topping the wide and flaring nostrils. The mouth was the biggest that Olaf had ever seen on a human face; the lips were thick, pursed, parted, showing snow-white teeth. The black neck was like a bull's . . . The giant advanced upon Olaf and stood over him.

"I want a bottle of whisky and a woman," he said. "Can you fix me up?"

"Yes," Olaf whispered, wild with anger and insult.

But what was he angry about? He's had requests like this

every night from all sorts of men and he was used to fulfilling them; he was a night porter in a cheap, water-front Copenhagen hotel that catered to sailors and students. Yes, men needed women, but this man, Olaf felt, ought to have a special sort of woman. He felt a deep and strange reluctance to phone any of the women whom he habitually sent to men. Yet he had promised. Could he lie and say that none was available? No. That sounded too fishy. The black giant sat upon the bed, staring straight before him. Olaf moved about quickly, pulling down the window shades, taking the pink coverlet off the bed, nudging the giant with his elbow to make him move as he did so . . . That's the way to treat 'im . . . Show 'im I ain't scared of 'im . . . But he was still seeking for an excuse to refuse. And he could think of nothing. He felt hypnotized, mentally immobilized. He stood hesitantly at the door.

"You send the whisky and the woman quick, pal?" the black giant asked, rousing himself from a brooding stare.

"Yes," Olaf grunted, shutting the door.

Goddamn, Olaf sighed He sat in his office at his desk before the phone. Why did he have to come here? . . . I'm not prejudiced . . . No, not at all . . . But . . . He couldn't think anymore. God oughtn't make men as big and black as that . . . But what the hell was he worrying about? He'd sent women of all races to men of all colors . . . So why not a woman to the black giant? Oh, only if the man were small, brown and intelligent-looking . . . Olaf felt trapped.

With a reflex movement of his hand, he picked up the phone and dialed Lena. She was big and strong and always cut him in for fifteen percent instead of the usual ten percent. Lena had four small children to feed and clothe.

Lena was willing, she was, she said, coming over right now. She didn't give a good goddamn about how big and black the man was . . .

"Why you ask me that?" Lena wanted to know over the phone. "You never asked that before . . ."

"But this one is *big*," Olaf found himself saying.

"He's just a man," Lena told him, her voice singing stridently, laughingly over the wire. "You just leave that to me. You don't have to do anything. *I'll* handle 'im."

Lena had a key to the hotel door downstairs, but tonight Olaf stayed awake. He wanted to see her. Why? He didn't know. He stretched out on the sofa in his office, but sleep was far from him. When Lena arrived, he told her again how big and black the man was.

"You told me that over the phone," Lena reminded him.

Olaf said nothing. Lena flounced off on her errand of mercy. Olaf shut the office door, then opened it and left it ajar. But why? He didn't know. He lay upon the sofa and stared at the ceiling. He glanced at his watch; it was almost two o'clock . . . She's staying in there a long time . . . Ah, God, but he could do with a drink . . . Why was he so damned worked up and nervous about a nigger and a white whore? . . . He'd never been so upset in all his life. Before he knew it, he had drifted off to sleep. Then he heard the office door swinging creakingly open on its rusty hinges Lena stood in it, frim and businesslike, her face scrubbed free of powder and rouge. Olaf scrambled to his feet, adjusting his eyeglasses, blinking.

"How was it?" he asked her in a confidential whisper.

Lena's eyes blazed.

"What the hell's that to you?" she snapped. "There's your cut," she said, flinging him his money, tossing it upon the covers of the sofa. "You're sure nosy tonight. You wanna take over my work?"

Olaf's pasty cheeks burned red.

"You go to hell," he said, slamming the door.

"I'll meet you there!" Lena's shouting voice reached him dimly.

He was being a fool; there was no doubt about it. But, try as he might, he could not shake off a primitive hate for that black mountain of energy, of muscle, of bone; he envied the easy manner in which it moved with such a creeping and powerful motion; he winced at the booming and commanding voice that came to him when the tiny little eyes were not even looking at him; he shivered at the sight of those vast and clawlike hands that seemed always to hint of death . . .

Olaf kept his counsel. He never spoke to Karen about the sordid doings at the hotel. Such things were not for women like Karen. He knew instinctively that Karen would have been amazed had he told her that he was worried sick about a nigger and a blonde whore . . . No; he couldn't talk to anybody about it, not even the hard-bitten old bitch who owned the hotel. She was concerned only about money; she didn't give a damn about how big and black a client was as long as he paid his room rent.

Next evening, when Olaf arrived for duty, there was no sight or sound of the black giant. A little later after one o'clock in the morning he appeared, left his key, and went out wordlessly. A few moments past two the giant returned, took his key from the board, and paused.

"I want that Lena again tonight. And another bottle of whisky," he said boomingly.

"I'll call her and see if she's in," Olaf said.

"Do that," the black giant said and was gone.

He thinks he's God, Olaf fumed. He picked up the phone and ordered Lena and a bottle of whisky, and there was a taste of ashes in his mouth. On the third night came the same request: Lena and whisky. When the black giant appeared on the fifth night, Olaf was about to make a sarcastic remark to the effect that maybe he ought to marry Lena, but he checked it in time . . . After all, he could kill me with one hand, he told himself.

Olaf was nervous and angry with himself for being nervous. Other black sailors came and asked for girls and Olaf sent them, but with none of the fear and loathing that he sent Lena and a bottle of whisky to the giant . . . All right, the black giant's stay was almost up. He'd said that he was staying for five or six nights; tomorrow night was the sixth night and that ought to be the end of this nameless terror.

On the sixth night Olaf sat in his swivel chair with his bottle of beer and waited, his teeth on edge, his fingers drumming the desk. But what the hell am I fretting for? . . . The hell with 'im . . . Olaf sat and dozed. Occasionally he'd awaken and listen to the foghorns of freighters sounding as ships came and went in the misty Copenhagen harbor. He was half asleep when he felt a rough hand on his shoulder. He blinked his eyes open. The giant, black and vast and powerful, all but blotted out his vision.

"What I owe you, man?" the giant demanded. "And I want my money."

"Sure," Olaf said, relieved, but filled as always with fear of this living wall of black flesh.

With fumbling hands, he made out the bill and received payment, then gave the giant his roll of money, laying it on the desk so as not to let his hands touch the flesh of the black mountain. Well, his ordeal was over. It was past two o'clock in the morning. Olaf even managed a wry smile and muttered a guttural "Thanks" for the generous tip that the giant tossed him.

Then a strange tension entered the office. The office door was shut and Olaf was alone with the black mass of power, yearning for it to leave. But the black mass of power stood still, immobile, looking down at Olaf. And Olaf could not, for the life of him, guess at what was transpiring in that mysterious black mind. The two of them simply stared at each other for a full two minutes, the giant's tiny little beady eyes blinking slowly as they seemed to measure and search Olaf's face. Olaf's vision dimmed for a second as terror seized him and he could feel a flush of heat overspread his body. Then Olaf sucked in his breath as the devil of blackness commanded:

"Stand up!"

Olaf was paralyzed. Sweat broke on his face. His worst premonitions about this black beast were coming true. This evil blackness was about to attack him, maybe kill him . . . Slowly

Olaf shook his head, his terror permitting him to breathe:

"What're you talking about?"

"Stand up, I say!: the black giant bellowed.

As though hypnotized, Olaf tried to rise; then he felt the black paw of the beast helping him roughly to his feet.

They stood an inch apart. Olaf's pasty-white features were lifted to the giant's swollen black face. The ebony ensemble of eyes and nose and mouth and cheeks looked down at Olaf, silently; then, with a low and deliberate movement of his gorillalike arms, he lifted his mammoth hands to Olaf's throat. Olaf had long known and felt that this dreadful moment was coming; he felt trapped in a nightmare. He could not move. He wanted to scream, but could find no words. His lips refused to open; his tongue felt icy and inert.

Then he knew that his end had come when the giant's black fingers slowly, softly encircled his throat while a horrible grin of delight broke out on the sooty face . . . Olaf lost control of the reflexes of his body and he felt a hot stickiness flooding his underwear . . . He stared without breathing, gazing into the grinning blackness of the face that was bent over him, feeling the black fingers caressing his throat and waiting to feel the sharp, stinging ache and pain of the bones in his neck being snapped, crushed . . . He knew all along that I hated 'im . . . Yes, and now he's going to kill me for it, Olaf told himself with despair.

The black fingers still circled Olaf's neck, not closing, but gently massaging it, as it were, moving to and fro, while the obscene face grinned into his. Olaf could feel the giant's warm breath blowing on his eyelashes and he felt like a chicken about to have its neck wrung and its body tossed to flip and flap dyingly in the dust of the barnyard . . . Then suddenly the black giant withdrew his fingers from Olaf's neck and stepped back a pace, still grinning. Olaf sighed, trembling, his body seeming to shrink; he waited. Shame sheeted him for the hot wetness that was in his trousers. Oh, God, he's teasing me . . . He's showing me how easily he can kill me . . . He swallowed, waiting, his eyes stones of gray.

The giant's barrel-like chest gave forth a low, rumbling chuckle of delight.

"You laugh?" Olaf asked whimperingly.

"Sure I laugh," the giant shouted.

"Please don't hurt me," Olaf managed to say.

"I wouldn't hurt you, boy," the giant said in a tone of mockery. "So long."

And he was gone. Olaf fell limply into the swivel chair and fought off losing consciousness. Then he wept. *He was showing me how easily he could kill me . . . He made me shake with terror and then laughed and left . . .* Slowly, Olaf recovered, stood, then gave vent to a string of curses:

"Goddamn 'im! My gun's right there in the desk drawer; I should of shot 'im. Jesus, I hope the ship he's on sinks . . . I hope he drowns and the sharks eat 'im . . ."

Later, he thought of going to the police, but sheer shame kept him back; and, anyway, the giant was probably on board his ship by now. And he had to get home and clean himself *Oh, Lord, what could he tell Karen?* Yes, he would say that his stomach had been upset . . . He'd change clothes and return to work. He phoned the hotel owner that he was ill and wanted an hour off; the old bitch said that she was coming right over and that poor Olaf could have the evening off.

Olaf went home and lied to Karen. Then he lay awake the rest of the night dreaming of revenge. He saw that freighter on which the giant was sailing; he saw it springing a dangerous leak and saw a torrent of sea water flooding, gushing into all the compartments of the ship until it found the bunk in which the black giant slept. Ah, yes, the foamy, surging waters would surprise that sleeping black bastard of a giant and he would drown, gasping and choking like a trapped rat, his tiny eyes bulging until they glittered red, the bitter water of the sea pounding his lungs until they ached and finally burst . . . The depths of the sea and a shark, a *white* one, would glide aimlessly about the shut portholes until it found an open one and it would slither inside and nose about until it found that swollen, rotting, stinking carcass of the black beast and it would then begin to nibble at the decomposing mass of tarlike flesh, eating the bones clean . . . Olaf always pictured the giant's bones as being jet black and shining.

Once or twice, during these fantasies of cannibalistic revenge, Olaf felt a little guilty about all the many innocent people, women and children, all white and blonde, who would have to go down into watery graves in order that that white shark could devour the evil giant's flack flesh . . . But, despite feelings of remorse, the fantasy lived persistently on, and when Olaf found himself alone, it would crowd and cloud his mind to the exclusion of all else, affording him the only revenge he knew. To make me suffer just for the pleasure of it, he fumed. Just to show me how strong he was . . . Olaf learned how to hate, and got pleasure out of it.

Summer fled on wings of rain. Autumn flooded Denmark with color. Winter made rain and snow fall on Copenhagen. Finally spring came, bringing violets and roses. Olaf kept to his job. For many months he feared the return of the black giant. But when a year had passed and the giant had not put in an appearance, Olaf allowed his revenge fantasy to peter out, indulging in it only when recalling the shame that the black monster had made him feel.

Then one rainy August night, a year later, Olaf sat drowsing at his desk, his bottle of beer before him, tilting back in his swivel chair, his feet resting atop a corner of his desk, his mind mulling over the more pleasant aspects of his life. The office door cracked open. Olaf glanced boredly up and around. His heart jumped and skipped a beat. The black nightmare of terror and shame that he had hoped that he had lost forever was again upon him . . . Resplendently dressed, suitcase in hand, the black looming mountain filled the doorway. Olaf's thin lips parted and a silent moan, half a curse, escaped them.

109

"Hy," the black giant boomed from the doorway.

Olaf could not reply. But a sudden resolve swept him: this time he would even the score. If this black beast came within so much as three feet of him, he would snatch his gun out of the drawer and shoot him dead, so help him God . . .

"No rooms tonight," Olaf heard himself announcing in a determined voice.

The black giant grinned; it was the same infernal grimace of delight and triumph that he had had when his damnable black fingers had been around his throat . . .

"Don't want no room tonight," the giant announced.

"Then what are you doing here?" Olaf asked in a loud but tremulous voice.

The giant swept toward Olaf and stood over him; and Olaf could not move, despite his oath to kill him . . .

"What do you want then?" Olaf demanded once more, ashamed that he could not lift his voice above a whisper.

The giant still grinned, then tossed what seemed the same suitcase upon Olaf's sofa and bent over it; he zippered it open with a sweep of his clawlike hand and rummaged in it, drawing forth a flat, gleaming white object done up in glowing cellophane. Olaf watched with lowered lids, wondering what trick was now being played on him. Then, before he could defend himself, the giant had whirled and again long, black, snakelike fingers were encircling Olaf's throat . . . Olaf stiffened, his right hand clawing blindly for the drawer where the gun was kept. But the giant was quick.

"Wait," he bellowed, pushing Olaf back from the desk.

The giant turned quickly to the sofa and, still holding his fingers in a wide circle that seemed a noose for Olaf's neck, he inserted the rounded fingers into the top of the flat, gleaming object. Olaf had the drawer open and his sweaty fingers were now touching his gun, but something made him freeze. The flat, gleaming object was a shirt and the black giant's circled fingers were fitting themselves into its neck . . .

"A perfect fit!" the giant shouted.

Olaf stared, trying to understand. His fingers loosened about the gun. A mixture of a laugh and a curse struggled in him. He watched the giant plunge his hands into the suitcase and pull out other flat, gleaming shirts.

"One, two, three, four, five, six," the black giant intoned, his voice crisp and businesslike. "Six nylon shirts. And they're all yours. One shirt for each time Lena came . . . See, Daddy-O?"

The black, cupped hands, filled with billowing nylon looked like snow in the dead of winter. Was this true? Could he believe it? Maybe this too was a trick? But, no. There were six shirts, all nylon, and the black giant had had Lena six nights.

"What's the matter with you, Daddy-O?" the giant asked. "You blowing your top? Laughing and crying . . ."

Olaf swallowed, dabbed his withered fists at his dimmed eyes; then he realized that he had his glasses on. He took them off and dried his eyes and sat up. He sighed, the tension and shame and fear and haunting dread of his fantasy went from him, and he leaned limply back in his chair . . ."

"Try one on," the giant ordered.

Olaf fumbled with the buttons of his shirt, let down his suspenders, and pulled the shirt off. He donned a gleaming nylon one and the giant began buttoning it for him.

"Perfect, Daddy-O," the giant said.

His spectacled face framed in sparkling nylon, Olaf sat with trembling lips. So he'd not been trying to kill me after all.

"You want Lena, don't you?" he asked the giant in a soft whisper. "But I don't know where she is. She never came back here after you left — "

"I know where Lena is," the giant told him. "We been writing to each other. I'm going to her house. And, Daddy-O, I'm late." The giant zippered the suitcase shut and stood a moment gazing down at Olaf, his tiny little red eyes blinking slowly. Then Olaf realized that there was a compassion in that stare that he had never seen before.

"And I thought you wanted to kill me," Olaf told him. "I was scared of you . . ."

"Me? Kill you?" the giant blinked. "When?"

"That night when you put your fingers about my throat."

"What?" the giant asked, then roared with laughter. "Daddy-O, you're a funny little man. I wouldn't hurt you. I like you. You a *good* man. You helped me."

Olaf smiled, clutching the pile of nylon shirts in his arms.

"You're a good man too," Olaf murmured. Then loudly: "You're a big black good man."

"Daddy-O, you're crazy," the giant said.

He swept his suitcase from the sofa, spun on his heel, and was at the door in one stride.

"Thanks!" Olaf cried after him.

The black giant paused, turned his vast black head, and flashed a grin.

"Daddy-O, drop dead," he said and was gone.

* * *

Richard Wright (1908 – 1960) was born on a plantation near Natchez, Mississippi. When he was eight his family moved to Arkansas and later to Jackson, Mississippi. At the age of fifteen (he was in the eighth grade) he published his first story, "The Voodoo of Hell's Half-Acre," in the *Southern Register*, a local newspaper. At the age of seventeen, he moved to Memphis, Tennessee, where he was soon joined by his mother and younger brother.

In 1937, Wright moved to New York and became the editor of the *Daily Worker*, a Communist newspaper. By 1938 he had gained a national reputation as a writer based on a collection of four short stories entitled *Uncle Tom's Children*. Two years later he published what is probably his best-known work, *Native Son*. The book was selected by the Book of the Month Club as its first offering by an African-American writer.

As an adult he lived in Montreal, Canada, before moving to Paris, where he became a French citizen in 1947. His most important books include *Native Son* (required reading in many high schools), *Eight Men*, and *Black Boy*. As a leading African-American intellectual he often has been compared to James Baldwin and Toni Morrison.

Ellen Gilchrist

A CHRISTMAS STORY

BY ELLEN GILCHRIST

It was late on Christmas Eve when Mary Anne Meredith Merryship was born, a long, skinny baby girl who came sliding out as if she were too fine to cause her mother trouble. Two hours after the water broke, one hour after they reached the Singing River Hospital in Ocean Springs, Mississippi, thirty minutes before Christmas Eve mass began at Saint Paul's Episcopal Church, where her six brothers knelt beside her aunts and uncles and grandparents, this unasked-for, unintended blessing slid down the birth canal and came out with her eyes wide open.

Somewhere in the background Pachelbel's Canon in D Major was playing softly. The obstetrician in attendance was a student of classical music and played it while she worked.

Usually babies were delivered in the rooms where their mothers were waiting but they had moved Meredith's mother into an operating room because the hospital was crowded with patients from the recent tornados in southern Mississippi.

"A girl," the doctor whispered to Anne Chautivan Merryship, who was her first cousin and should have had more sense than to have another baby at her age. "At last, Annie, you have a girl."

"I told you," Anne said, giggling, excited. "Give her to me." In a moment the baby girl was in her arms, looking up at her with eyes as green as the sea. "It was hard not telling you she was a girl," her cousin-doctor said. "Hard not telling Daniel." She bent over her cousin-patient, finished her work, and began pulling off her gloves. "Where is Daniel?"

"Getting batteries for Christmas toys. We didn't think it would be so soon." Anne kept her eyes on her daughter. For six months she had put up with the frowns and innuendos of her family and her friends, even Daniel had not been as enthusiastic as she was, and only two of the children had shown any real interest. This baby girl was hers. "A gift I never would have given myself," she said many times that long summer and fall while everyone else thought she was crazy.

The little boys were twelve, eleven, ten, eight, six and four. The old Victorian house Anne and Daniel had rebuilt had rooms for every child. The baby girl would have to have an upstairs linen pantry or stay in her parents' room for several years. None of that mattered. She was here, a green-eyed baby girl named Mary Anne Meredith Merryship, after two great-grandmothers and an aunt. These were the three who had shared Anne's excitement over another baby, or, at least, had had the grace to pretend it was a fine idea.

Anne's husband, Daniel, was hurrying into the room, wearing a gown and cap. "I'm so sorry," he began.

"Mary Anne Meredith Merryship," Anne said. "Meet your green-eyed daughter."

"Oh, my," he leaned down to kiss them both. Daniel was a dentist. He worked five days a week from eight in the morning until six at night. He was good at what he did. He was almost out of debt. All the children were healthy and strong. He took joy in them. When things got tight Grandmother Meredith could always bail them out. Things didn't get too tight anymore. He was sought out. He had to turn away patients. It would be all right. It was always all right.

"I love you," he said. "And I love her too. Are you sure she wants all that name?"

"If she stops liking it, we'll have it changed. Look at how sweet she is. Look at her hair. That's a lot of hair for a newborn baby."

"It sure is. It's the most hair I've ever seen."

"Go tell the boys. Go to mass. You can still get there for the end. I want them to know while they are there so they can say a prayer for her."

"You are a prayer," he heard himself say. It was not the sort of thing he said. Maybe it was the music. Pachelbel's Canon in D Major.

* * *

In the church the little boys were lined up in between their Aunt Mary and their Uncle Philip. Charles and Michael had kicked each other a few times but aside from that they had been very well behaved. It was a strange Christmas. For one thing there was a full moon. For another thing it was fifty degrees outside, cold for December in Ocean Springs. Driving down the beach on their way to church their uncle had rolled down all the windows so they could see the moonlight on the beach and the Mississippi Sound.

"Tonight you are having a baby just like Jesus was born in Nazareth," He said. "There's a big star near the moon if you look for it. When we get out we'll look for it and see if we can see it."

"And the three wise men and their camels are coming down the beach to get to the hospital to see our baby when it gets here," Sean said. He was ten and took everything very seriously.

"But our Momma is going to have a baby sister," four-year-old Charles said. "She said she was trying to get a girl baby but she might get a boy. I want a boy so he can be in my room."

"That's really weird," eight-year-old Rafael said. "This baby is coming at the same time as Santa Claus."

"He believes in Santa Claus," twelve-year-old Martin said. "He's such a baby."

"Shut up, Martin," their Uncle Philip said. "It's a holy night. Let go all that sarcasm for the night." He reached across the seat and patted Martin on the knee. Uncle Philip was the oldest of his family. He knew how Martin felt. When his mother had babies he had always thought she was a fool. Well, his sister-in-law was a fool to have all these children but they liked them and didn't want to give any of them back, so that was pretty much that about his sister-in-law, Anne, and her choices, if they were choices. She was an only child. It was deeper than choices. Philip was a psychologist. He mostly treated disturbed teenage boys.

He dealt with alcohol and drug addiction, crazy parents, problems no one could really fix. He did what he could. It had made him cynical and sleepless. It made him constantly on watch where his nephews were concerned. It made him think Anne didn't understand a thing to have another baby at a time when the boys were reaching puberty. Oh, well, he thought, we'll all pitch in, we'll fix it.

"Come talk to me about this baby if it bothers you," he said to Martin, the sarcastic twelve year old. "It's all right to be upset by it, to think it's stupid. I thought Grandmother Anne was out of her mind when she kept having my brothers."

"I don't care one way or the other," Martin said. "As long as I don't have to take care of it."

"Let's go out on my boat next week," Philip said. "We can go out to Horn Island and build a fire. Maybe spend the night.

We haven't done it in awhile."

"In this cold weather?"

"It will get warmer. This won't last."

* * *

They pulled up to the side of Saint Paul's and the boys got out and went to the front of the church to wait for their Aunt Mary and their Aunt Lane.

Inside candles were burning and the choir was lining up for the processional. Even Martin was taken in by the holy feeling of Christmas Eve. The music began, the organ played the first notes of the first hymn, THE CHURCH'S ONE FOUNDATION IS JESUS CHRIST OUR LORD. The family moved together, Charles and Michael stopped kicking each other and Uncle Philip put his arm around his nephew Martin and kept it there.

The service was more than half over when their father slipped into the pew behind them and began to whisper to them that they had a baby sister. He told his brother Philip last and Philip felt a strange, weird happiness at the thought of his sister-in-law having a daughter. He was surprised at his pleasure.

* * *

At the hospital Anne's grandmother Meredith came into the room where her oldest granddaughter and only great-granddaughter were cuddled up in a bed behind a curtain in a shared room with a fourteen-year-old boy who had broken his leg in the tornado in D'Iberville in early December. His parents were with him behind their curtains but his lovely tall mother had poked her head around Anne's curtain to tell her Merry Christmas and congratulations.

"Do you want to look at her?" Anne asked, and the woman said yes and moved gingerly toward the bed and looked down at the baby and began to cry. Small, soft tears.

"I'm sorry," she said. "It's just such a lovely, lovely thing. A baby girl at Christmas. What is her name?"

"Mary Anne Meredith Merryship. If she doesn't like it she can change it."

"Merry Christmas, Mary Anne Meredith Merryship," the woman said. "Thanks for coming to cheer us up."

She went back behind her curtains to her son. Anne looked at her mother and her grandmother and said, "See, she is already spreading joy around the world."

Her mother got up and went to the bed and kissed her daughter. "I'm sorry I wasn't more enthusiastic," she said. "I just get so worried every time you have a baby. I think something will go wrong. I think you will be harmed."

"Nothing went wrong, Momma. She just slid out. You all don't need to stay. I'm going to sleep in awhile. The nurses are here. Daniel will be back in the morning. I wanted him to stay with the boys. Take Grandmother home. It's too late for her to be up."

"No it isn't," Grandmother Meredith said, "It's good for old people to have excitement. I have waited a long time for a namesake. Let me see her again. Then we will go home and let you sleep. She moved near the bed and adjusted her glasses and looked deep into the face of the unexpected, uninvited, unintended blessing of a child. "She looks exactly like me," Grandmother Meredith declared. "That child is my spitting image as I will prove to you as soon as I get out my photograph albums." She was laughing then as she was a lighthearted, laughing grandmother who had given birth to lighthearted, laughing sons who mostly had lighthearted children, but not always. Her granddaughter Anne was not lighthearted. She
was a serious, ambitious girl who had grown into a woman who did whatever she set out to do and did it well.

Grandmother Meredith slipped a small gift-wrapped box into her granddaughter's free hand. "It's for her," she said. "I've known for months she was a girl."

"How did you know?" Anne was smiling and laughing. Her grandmother could always do that to her. You never knew when she was teasing you.

"I got it out of your cousin Katherine when I went in for my checkup in September. I kept begging her to tell me and finally she did. She didn't exactly say it but she wouldn't say no, it wasn't a girl, so I have known all those months and only told one other person, well, two other people."

"Who did you tell?" Anne was really laughing now.

"My cousin Nell who lives in Indiana. You know Nell, she used to come and visit when she could travel. And I told my hairdresser, Rosie, at Tips, Toes and Tresses. She barely speaks English so I thought it was safe to tell her. Well, I also told the lady who gives me manicures, but she only speaks Vietnamese. Rosie had to translate."

Anne shifted the baby into her left arm so she could open the small package. It was Grandmother Meredith's engagement ring, a diamond solitaire in a Tiffany setting.

"Oh, my," she said.

"They won't even like them by the time she grows up," Grandmother Meredith said. "She'll probably sell it to buy some new sort of cellular telephone. Anyway, maybe you can wear it until she grows up."

Anne's mother was shaking her head and trying not to cry. The woman in the next cubicle was listening and putting her head through the curtains, the nurse was coming in the room to send the visitors home, and two miles away the six little boys and their aunts and uncles were standing in front of the church looking up at the cold, clear sky and the huge moon and the correct sort-of looking star, which was actually the planet Venus.

"Mary Anne Meredith Merryship," Martin was saying to his grandfather Philip. "That is about the stupidest thing I've ever heard of anyone naming a baby. It's bad enough we have to have this last name without making a joke out of it and putting it on some helpless little girl when she goes to school. I'm going to call her Noel. It means the same thing."

"Great idea," his Uncle Philip said. "Can you believe men walked on that," he continued, pointing at the moon. "We sat down here in Ocean Springs, Mississippi on the hottest day in July and had a party that lasted until four in the morning to watch on television while men walked on the moon."

"They will do it again," his father Philip said. "It will probably be the Chinese this time, but they'll be there. Would you want to do it, Martin?"

"No, I want to be the Governor of Mississippi so I can make laws and keep people from being so crazy."

"Good idea," his Uncle Philip said. "Of course you have to start with yourself so you will know how hard that is to do."

Charles, age four, and Michael, age six, came up to their uncle and their father and began to ask the real question of the night.

"Can Santa Claus get in to leave our presents if we never go to bed?" Michael asked. "Me and Charles want to go home and go to sleep."

* * *

The aunts and uncles and their father, Daniel, and their Uncle Philip and their grandfather Philip piled the children into two cars and took them home and put them into bed.

Uncle Philip stayed with his brother Daniel to put the batteries into the presents and do all the other secret, holy things grown people have to do while they wait for Santa Claus.

"Where is my Momma?" Charles asked as he went to sleep in the double bed with Michael.

"She's at the hospital getting the baby girl," Michael said. "It was inside her and now it's out. She'll be home tomorrow. Act like you like the baby whether you do or not."

"How does she get it out?" Charles asked, remembering a

movie about an alien he was not supposed to watch at his cousin's house but watched anyway. "Like Alien, like in that?"

"Of course not," Michael said. "Our cousin Katherine has a way to get it out and then they have to clean it up and put on a dress and give it a shot and then they can bring it home. I saw you right after you got out. You looked pretty good. The first thing they did was give you a shot. I couldn't look. I told Daddy they shouldn't do that to brand new babies but he said they had to."

He looked beside him to see what Charles thought of this terrible revelation but Charles had fallen asleep. Michael fell asleep too, thinking how he had promised Jesus in church he would not kick Charles anymore even if Charles kicked him first. Michael heaved a sleepy sigh remembering what a terrible thing it had been for them to give Charles a shot when he had just gotten out and was more determined than ever to stop kicking him all the time. Even if he kicks me first, Michael determined. I'll just grab his foot and hold it so he can't do it anymore. He fell asleep thinking about holding Charles' foot and managed to forget about how terrible it was to watch a tiny baby get a shot.

* * *

Born in 1935 in Vicksburg, Mississippi, Ellen Gilchrist attended Millsaps College in Jackson, Mississippi, where she studied creative writing under Eudora Welty, and subsequently did postgraduate study at the University of Arkansas in Fayetteville, where she is currently a professor of creative writing at the university. She maintains homes in both Ocean Springs, Mississippi, and Fayetteville, Arkansas.

Gilchrist published her first novel, *The Annunciation*, in 1983 and followed that with her second collection of short stories, *Victory Over Japan*, which won the 1984 American Book Award for fiction. She has won acclaim for her poetry, but it is her short stories for which she is best known. In 2004 she received the fifth annual Thomas Wolfe Prize from the University of North Carolina. **From 1984 to 1985, Gilchrist** was a commentator on National Public Radio's *Morning Edition*. Her NPR commentaries subsequently were published in a book titled *Falling Through Space*. Interestingly, Gilchrist did not publish her first book until she was in her forties.

Willie Morris / photo by James L. Dickerson for the Greenwood *Commonwealth*
Used with permission

LUKE AND THE LEGIONNAIRES

BY WILLIE MORRIS

"At night the heart comes out," the poet from Wales wrote, "like a cat on the tiles." It was a mellifluous twilight, soft and shimmering pink—a midsummer's night, heavy-sweet with clover and tuberoses and the lingering honeysuckle. Georgia and Arch and I were going to a movie (we called it then a "show"), and to while away the time until they arrived I was sitting on the front steps watching cars go by and reflecting on Mr. Leroy Godbold in the courtroom. People would slow down and wave and shout "*Swayze!*" letting the word roll out long and liltingly as was the custom.

A crew of older boys from the high school came by in a battered prewar Mercury convertible and gave me the finger. Mrs. Idella King, the high school English teacher drove past, so myopic and of such wandering disposition that she was constantly running into things, a parked fire truck or the mosquito conveyance, and when I sighted one of the neighborhood boys bicycling several feet from her I closed my eyes, but she missed him. The tap dancing had shut down for the day, and my mother was across the street prattling with two skeletal spinster sisters in their eighties, who claimed they never married because all the available men were lost in that early war, the Civil War, though I always suspected other more obvious reasons.

The boulevard kids were already congregating down the way to "play out," as it was called, in those sibilant evenings — run barefoot in the cool wet grass to the symphony of the crickets and cicadas, gather fireflies in jelly jars, scare one another in the delicious horrors of the shadows — just as we had done, especially around the looming old Darnell house ten doors down, hidden now in indolent crape myrtles and elms and a giant cucumber tree, where an ancient widow named Alabama Darnell, whom we hardly ever saw, dwelled alone with a nearly ancient mulatto named Isabella, a striking duenna. One night like this when we were little and Mars was close to the earth, we all kept gazing into the cloud-laden skies, up where people had said it would be. The clouds cleared, and there was Mars itself, and from our earthly nimbus we took turns looking at it through a cheap set of binoculars. Was anyone there at all? Did they play football on Mars?

Now the boulevard rang with the ineffable sounds of children at play. A group of six or seven black children came along the sidewalk pushing a worn-out tire; then scampering and chattering, they took the shortcut through our driveway and the line of pecan trees to Independence Quarters. From the house next door Mrs. Griffin was playing the piano; I could picture her wan and proud and thin in her heavy eyeglasses, poised at her keyboard in waxen gentility. Her repertoire consisted of Kern and Romberg. "Smoke Gets in Your Eyes" and "Ten Thousand Men" were her contributions to this fine summer solstice.

From the beer place in the Quarters rose the resonant illicit laughter that always attended the gathering dusks, and then the sonorous cadences of "Sharecropper's Blues" and "Dust My

127

Broom" blending shamelessly with "Indian Love Call" and "On the Road to Mandalay."

Along the boulevard men in shirtsleeves were watering their lawns. Never mind the stout rains of three days before, or that the lawns themselves seemed lush enough now to outlast any summer. The gentle wheeze of two dozen hoses joined in with the pulsing life.

In that moment, as the children next door shrieked at some obscure horror, Luke Cartwright came to a halt at the front curb. I watched as he got out of his truck and came toward me with his slow, loping strides.

"It's me," he said, and sat down on the steps.

He wore khakis and tanned leather work boots with strands of wet Johnson grass stuck to them and a green work cap with the words "John Deere" on the front. His face was deep bronze from the sun, but his nose and ears and the backs of his hands were blistered red. He gently touched his nose, as if to ascertain whether there were any feeling left in it.

"I been working on the vegetables at the farm," he said.

He reached down and patted Dusty on the head. "How old's the dog?"

"Six and a half."

I would not have been surprised if he had replied, "That's old enough," as he had to me on our first encounter. But instead, he said, "I understand you and Georgia went to the trial today."

We saw the end, I said.

"Why did you go?" Georgia shouldn't go. Maybe *you* ought to be there, but not her."

Well, we go sometimes.

"What was Old Man Godbold up to?"

I was tempted to describe everything I had seen from the gallery, the imperial presence of him, the jurors, the witnesses, the sheriff and his men, but merely told him that Mr. Godbold seemed interested in everything.

With this he bent down and picked a long blade of grass by the side of the steps, which he put between his lips. He looked across the boulevard toward my mother and the spinster siblings, who were conversing as animatedly as ever.

"I just bet he was."

We sat there for a while absorbing the sounds of the neighborhood. It was nearly dark now. Suddenly, as if the conductor of a philharmonic orchestra had brought down his baton with a bold emphatic flourish, every katydid in Fisk's Landing began to sing.

This odd man of truncated queries and unembarrassed silences and the quizzical, good-natured face never seemed in a hurry for anything. I suspected he would tell me why he came by when he felt like it. Only when I really grew to know him did I comprehend that for him words were too valuable to squander and that one might just as well use them forthrightly. Not that he could not talk when he was of the mood. As I would discover, he was occasionally given to sudden observations that may have had little to do with the subject at hand; this quirk led me to suspect that when he was alone he talked to himself the way I talked to my dog.

"Sometimes it only takes about ten seconds to tell someone's a real ass," he might say, or "Weddings are harder than funerals," or "This town is five thousand swamp rats and five thousand hillbillies, and fifty Jews and eighty Episcopalians." His speech included bizarre rhetorical flourishes: "His crop is always good because he has ice cream land'" or "That farm's so poor a crow won't fly over it" or "She applied a tin bucket to his ears" or "The woman has snakes in her head" or "She's so ugly she'll kill young cotton."

All this he delivered in a strong, throaty voice that was often so low you had to bend an ear to listen, and punctuated, sometimes surprisingly, by a funny, high-pitched, infectious giggle.

He habitually lapsed into the quintessential vernacular in his pronunciations. For instance, although he certainly knew better, it was every now and again not *once*, but *onct*; a baseball inning could be an *ending*, *chaperon* might be *chaferon*, and *business* because *bidness*. Serviceable *ain'ts* and flamboyant double negative and ill-matched verbs and subjects and dubious tenses and comical ellipses were more faithful and efficacious than the most refined of Latinates. Consistency in speech was never his goal, and he moved at will from the most backwoods dialect to the King's English.

Then there was the way he used the word *nigger*, a generic and earthy word to us in those unenlightened times; unlike most others who used the word, Luke delivered it so simply and naturally and bereft of meanness or hostility that with him the word itself somehow suggested a realistic and almost benign and even affectionate recognition of the hard fraternity of shared land and its people, our mutual heritage and fate.

On the surface, then, he was a simple and bucolic fellow, a creature of his Spartan-hard heritage, a funny, grumpy, iconoclastic guy. But as it turned out, he was much more complicated than that. It took me a very long time to see that he was also an ironic man, full of surprises, and achingly American. Much as he loved the playfulness of life, more than almost any person I would ever know, he sensed the essential malevolence of things and aberrant behavior and people's limitations. He despised cruelty, but suffered buffoons.

Do you have to know pain to know compassion? He would exchange intelligence with nearly anybody about anything, usually in a terse shorthand—the boll weevil, baseball, local history, veterinary medicine—and old-fashioned Jeffersonian if ever there was one.

He was always looking at things, clouds, trees, hills, grass, dogs, birds, people, as if they might vanish swiftly in a puff.

He was half redneck and half coat-and-tie, half flatland and half hills, not four years at the aristocratic state university but two, handsome yet with the hard, callused hands of a yeoman, so that the very dichotomy of our land itself, its warring and contradictory imperatives, were who Luke was. One of his salvations, I would learn, was that he knew this about himself, and it must have amused him. More important, I think, all this had to do with pride and survival and remembrance and honor and right and wrong and the things that mattered. I would grow to love him very much.

"Well, we need you day after tomorrow," he finally said.

I asked who it was.

"Scuttles."

I paused as before to envision him.

"A good boy," he said. "Didn't talk much, as I recall. Didn't know much of nothing. Mortar got him."

My dog had left us to sprawl on the lawn and rub his back in the grass. He lay there will all four paws extended in the air, then got up to investigate some children in a tree next door. Mrs. Griffin was playing louder than ever, and was signing now to her own notes, and the two of us sat there for a moment listening to her. "Give me some men who are stouthearted men, and I'll soon give you ten thousand more."

Porter Ricks and Woodrow had met the coffin that afternoon at the railroad station in Monroe City, he said. "They shipped it all the way from Frisco to Brooklyn and then down here. All up and down the United States. You'd think they'd make it more *direct*, wouldn't you? Leave that to the army. I wouldn't be surprised if Scuttles had ended up in Mexico."

He was quiet, then said: "It's getting' worse. You know that? Arch Kidd's back, ain't he? I thought I saw him yesterday."

I told him he would be along at any moment.

The funeral would be at 3:00 in the new section. "We'll do

it right this time, echo too. Be there early like before. You can fill Arch in."

I already had.

"Good."

At this precise instant the black and white Plymouth came to a halt behind Luke's truck. Arch was at the wheel and Georgia next to him. Luke and I went out to greet them. He stopped at the window. "How are you on the high F?"

"The high F?" Arch asked. "On *what?*"

"On 'Taps.'"

"I'm great on the high F."

"See you day after tomorrow then," he said, and with a superfluous half wave departed.

I got in the car next to them. Arch negotiated the U-turn toward downtown, and I watched apprehensively as my mother disengaged herself from the spinsters and rushed to the curb. "Where are you goin?" she shouted. "What time are you coming back? Be careful!"

Later that night the three of us lingered for a while on Georgia's lawn. In the sultry sky there was a glossy little moon, as thin as the tiniest saucer, but storm clouds were gathering again like snowbanks along the horizon, and a sudden flank of lightning illuminated the grove of oaks on the school grounds, and the spray from it chased us onto the porch. Inside, I could see Georgia's parents watching their new television. The flickering images cast a pallid glow on the shrubbery outside and on the tall white columns of the gallery.

As the three of us stood there, Arch reached in his pocket and brought out a quarter. He polished it dramatically on his sleeve.

"Here," he said to her, "You flip it."

She held it in her fingers.

"You call it," Arch said.

"Heads," I said, as she tossed it in the air and slapped it

briskly on her forearm. "Heads," she said.

* * *

There was a small oblique rainfall, a warm summer rain as shy as tears, when Arch came to get me the next day. I had left the house early and was hiding in the bushes next to the Griffin residence to avoid my mother's hairbrush. I waited there amid the gnats and flies. When I saw the car, I burst from the shrubbery with my trumpet case in hand and hailed him down.

"What was *that* for?"

He was wearing a dark blue suit and matching tie, silver cufflinks and black shoes and socks. I, in salubrious, contrast, wore blue jeans and a T-shirt and white athletic socks and crimson sneakers with "F.L.H.S." stenciled on them. I did not envy him his chafing wardrobe on such a day, and certainly not the sobering rite awaiting him at the gravesite.

I was not nearly so nervous as the first time, when I was alone, but as we approached the cemetery I noted an irritable tenseness in Arch's silences, and in the elusive drops of perspiration on his upper lip.

"Do you know how long to wait before the echo?" he asked.

About four or five seconds.

"Where exactly do I stand at this thing, for Chrissake?"

"I'll show you."

The tombstones in the old section were etched somberly against the inconstant rain, gray against gray, in the ponderous afternoon. We followed the road through the Catholic enclave in back, then crossed the precarious divide of dark slopes and ravines into the new section. There were not many graves in this recent addition.

The Ricks Funeral Home canopy stood at that very spot where the clusters of new stones abruptly ended before the vaster emptiness beyond. The funeral home van and Luke

Cartwright's truck had already arrived .We parked farther up the hill near a young mimosa tree and got out with our horns.

In this new setting the site and all its accoutrements were a replica of that first burial: The Ricks van, the forbidding aperture in the earth, the mechanical lowering device, the bright green artificial grass, the funeral home chairs. When Arch and I reached the grave he began investigating. As the rain tapped eerily on the roof of the canopy, he looked down into the gaping hole.

"Oh, *shit!*"

Luke in his blue and gold Legion cap and gray suit had been walking among the newest graves. Now he and I showed Arch where to stand He took out a handkerchief and wiped the rain from his trumpet. After that he inserted the mouthpiece and started doing the scales. I took my own trumpet and ran up and down the scales also.

This sudden cacophony, tuneless and perfunctory, drew the gravediggers hidden in a shroud of mimosas down the way to come out and watch, and the venerable sexton, Chase Bowie, too, walked over. Mr. Bowie looked especially thin and stooped on this day. He wore starched khakis and a broad straw hat pulled down almost to his eyes; raindrops dripped from the brim. His cheek bulged with a modest plug of tobacco. As he joined Luke and me, the two of them silently gazed out at the acres of green, empty ground.

"Lots of space here, Mr. Bowie," Luke said.

"Yes, sir. Big enough for the next two, I'd guess."

"Two *what?*"

"Generations." He gently spat.

"The economy ain't been good," Luke said with a sly glance. "How come you're *expanding?*"

"It comes in spurts. Not a one last week. Four put down out here the week before. But it's a pretty steady business."

Then, just as before, the ageless red sedan with the American Legionnaires sped up the hill in our direction. They climbed out in their customary flurry of activity, shouting salutations to Luke. They fetched their carbines from the trunk and stood there testing the bolts.

"I think I found you the spot," Luke said. "Come see what you think. They'll be here in a few minutes." As we left the gravesite, Arch was standing in sartorial display under the tent, his back to the grave, as dejected as I had ever seen him. "See you in a little while," I said. Where was his irascibility now?

We climbed the vacant slopes to a dense thicket of red oaks and hickories far above the grave; their broad, heavy branches deflected the rain.

"What do you think? They're not supposed to see you," Luke said.

It looked good to me.

"Here. Dry yourself off." He handed me a red bandanna. I rubbed the moisture from my face, then from the trumpet. We stood there for a moment. Far below was the town again, under the dismal skies a glimmering diagram on its hills and flat places. Farther out still, the great flatness seemed a timeless sea in the mist.

"Pretty, ain't it?" he said. And he was gone.

It is easy to see why one would hope every time for echo. Two or three times that summer I even prayed, "Lord, grant me the toss." I wished the Book of Common Prayer had yet another perspicacious invocation: "For those in Need of the Right Coin Flip."

Standing all alone now, the rain swishing peacefully in the leaves, the trees like amiable guardians above me, I could almost hear the beating of my own heart. I had everything to myself, the giant sweep of the sky, the softly sloping earth, the whole green world.

I withdrew the mouthpiece from the trumpet and began buzzing into it. I emptied the spit valve again. And then I saw the funeral cortege coming up the road of the old section, mournful and slow, the hearse and the cars and the pickup trucks, weaving among the stones in serpentine dignity.

As it gradually approached the canopy, Arch and the Legionnaires came to attention. The pallbearers brought out the flag-draped coffin and carried it to the grave, and Potter Ricks and the official army escort guided the family to the chairs. Then the others came up and encircled them.

From my eminence I watched the service, a pantomime from where I was, a simple folk tableau with only the earth as the stage. Even the faint sounds of weeping wafted up to me, a nimble consonance from this distance, like the murmur of mourning doves at dusk, or the breathless flow of water in a summer's stream. Soon the Legionnaires fired their guns, and the sound boomed mightily across the woods. Then Arch began his notes, and they were firm and clear—until he missed the high F!

I waited for the notes to drift away, then put my lips to the mouthpiece and began. I got it right. And I felt for the first time the wonderful thrill of hearing the echo to one's *own* echo as it dissolves tenderly, reluctantly almost, into the distance, palpitating into the faraway hush.

I paused a few minutes for the mourners to disperse and then walked down the hill. The rain felt good on my face. The gravediggers were leaning on their shovels waiting for the last car to leave. Woodrow was folding the chairs. The smell of the flowers was cloyingly sweet as before, and Arch looked unwell. He had unbuttoned his collar and loosened his tie and was standing under the canopy as the gravediggers withdrew the fake grass and settled down to work. With the first thud of the dirt on the coffin Arch swiftly came out into the rain. Rarely had I seen him move so fast.

"The dead guy's mother drove me crazy," he whispered to me. "Could you *hear* her?"

As before, Potter Ricks was overseeing the tasks. "Good job, boys," he said to us as he came up to confer with the gravediggers. Arch, of course, did not say anything about the high note. I knew his pride had taken an irredeemable blow. If I had been the one, I would not have heard the end of it.

* * *

Luke found me in my backyard shooting baskets late the next afternoon. There would be a funeral the following day at 4:00 in a rural cemetery called Locust Grove. It was hard to find, Luke said. He had borrowed a station wagon, and he and the other Legionnaires would pick up Arch and me in front of my house at two. He promised to talk to our employer at the Jitney Jungle right away.

Arch and I worked that morning at the store. During a lull he motioned to me from the back. He was standing behind the meat counter next to Kinsey, a Negro boy two years our senior who played quarterback and ran and kicked for Number Two high school. He presided over the panoply of meat at the store, moving about on light nimble feet, which gave him a sort of gliding gait. Tall and fleet and sly, he had heavy-lidded eyes that read the slightest undue movement or unexpected nuance. His father was a carpenter, his mother a washerwoman, and there were ten siblings. Sometimes, during lapses in the commerce, Kinsey would be seen leaning on the counter studying hand-me-down textbooks from our school, as he was now.

"Here, Kinsey, Arch said, handing him a 50-cent piece.

I had been dreading this all day.

"What's this for?" Kinsey asked. He gazed at Arch obliquely, as if sensing some subtle betrayal. How could we have known then that in four years he would be the first-team running back for, of all places, the University of Illinois?

"We just want you to flip it."

"Tails," Arch said.

Kinsey looked briefly at each of us, tossed the coin high in the air, and slapped it into his open palm. It was tails.

The big thermometer in front of the bank registered 105 degrees that afternoon, making me yearn for the recent rains. On the thoroughfares of the town the asphalt seethed with black tar bubbles, the kind I tried to run my bicycle over when I was younger. On the drive out, the heat was so unbearable that my dress shirt became damp. The heavens were like hot brass, the sullen countryside soundless except for the wooden staccato of a pecker on a distant tree.

The narrow mazy road led past tangled woodland and gullies and ravines and patchy hills of cotton and corn and hay. The mindless kudzu sculptured the landscape, shrouding the hills and trees and telephone poles and vacant dwellings in crazy creeping green.

One farmer claimed he once saw kudzu growing all over a lazy cow. The tiny crossroads hamlets with their "Jesus Saves!" and "Prepare for Thy God" signs and decrepit grocery stories — unpainted establishments covered with chewing tobacco and cigar and soft drink advertisements and hand-drawn "No Cussin" and "Do Not Spit on Floor" posters — languished in this wicked inferno, and the old men sat lifeless on the front steps and porches, too torpid even to glance at us as we sped by.

We passed a pond dappled with cottonwood fluff and long stretches rampant with shortleaf pine and hardwood. The hilly countryside was dotted with tin-roofed dogtrot cabins, made of plank weatherboarding, and dusty yards full of chickens and dogs and clothes drying on fences and deteriorated houses resonant of the past and the people who once lived in them.

Arch, sitting next to me on the backseat of the station wagon behind Luke and the Legionnaires, looked dauntlessly cool and smug in his thin khakis and short-sleeved cotton shirt and saddle oxfords, and he sat there uncharacteristically prim with his trumpet case on his lap.

I gazed at the backs of the veterans' weathered necks. Although they talked now and then to Luke or among themselves, they too seemed beaten and subdued by the elements.

"Sarge" Jennings, as he was commonly known, had had to sell his farm for a pittance during the Depression and labored now behind the beer-and-soda counter at Crenshaw's Drug Store on the main street. Wash Rose was a used-car salesman. Cotton Ledbetter was a farmer who had once worked for Mr. Leroy Godbold. Roach Weems was a fireman. Fabian "Whiskey" Tubbs had the feed-and-seed store. Son Graham owned a small grocery on the fringes of the boulevard. They had been around so long, indeed, that they called the gravel road we were on a "rock road," and they all had stories, which more often than not they told.

Sarge Jennings won the Silver Star for valor in the First World War. This provost of pain and distress, of lantern jaw and burly rhythms, was one of the most perceptive observers among the Legionnaires, and I would come to know him well. With his epigrammatic and elemental speech, he had a poet's heart, although he would never have confessed to that. He was a tall, full-stomached figure of oaken constitution, with a bulbous red nose, spindly legs, speculating almond-shaped eyes, a leathery face that sometimes seemed unexpectedly young after a few neat swallows of Jim Beam, a slow, weighty voice, and dark graying hair so abundant that he could not get his ceremonial Legion cap over all of it, and it poked out around the sides and looked comical even in the most sorrowful moments.

The Sarge, like Arch and Luke, never went to any church and never wore a suit and tie except for burials. He was usually found at his station behind Crenshaw's long counters moving incessantly back and forth in brown boots and faded khakis and flowery multicolored shirts. He was a chain smoker of Chesterfields and judge of bourbon whiskey and a liberal fount of florid words, who knew the town as well as Potter Ricks or Luke did. He had single-handedly wiped out
a German machine-gun nest and saved the lives of at least five of his comrades — New England boys — in the blasted Argonne earth, but he never talked about that.

Wash Rose had his thumb and index finger shattered in the wheat fields near the Marne. Cotton Ledbetter nearly died of a lung wound at Soissons. Roach Weems acquired his name, as the others would explain (which they did often and with embellishment when the bottles were passed), for scurrying like a roach in the western front muck and the shredded Somme wilderness when the cannonade came in. Small and wizened like an aging mouse, lips so thin that in dry weather they nearly disappeared, and bald to his ears, he was as tough and lean as a sliver of Johnson grass. He was wary of strangers, and according to Sarge Jennings, had whipped men twice his size in crap-game fights, and probably could still, but he had mellowed a lot since '18. He sometimes said in his high-pitched voice, "I'm just *Roach*, Swayze."

The World War II men like Luke, who had chosen the Legion over the newer Veterans of Foreign Wars (Coach Asphalt Thomas, for instance, had picked the V.F.W.), were gradually assuming the leadership of the town post, but the survivors of the earlier combat seemed united in a warm, heightened camaraderie, as if that might have been the last American war that men could talk about when they came home. They had three or four favorite gathering spots. One was the little rectangular-frame Legion Hut at the upper end of the main street across from the grammar school, where, in a province nominally dedicated to legal prohibition of the meaner spirits, they had their own privately stocked bar, for in this hard-drinking society the old veterans were the hardest of the hard, and there was a garishly lighted jukebox from the Depression era, and they brought their wives here for monthly parties.

Crenshaw's Drug Store with its sign in front, "Come in or we'll both starve," was another of the places the veterans liked to congregate. The appellation drugstore was the most facile of overtures, for it dealt in condoms, laxatives, talcums, aspirins, and the more indigenous of the patent cures but not much else.

"The niggers come in when their nature's getting' weak,"

Sarge Jennings said. This anomalous institution consisted of two lengthy counters facing each other and separated by a soiled grungy interior area perhaps six or eight feet wide. The white men sat at one of the counters drinking their beer or soft drinks; the black men sat at the other facing the whites. The stamped tin ceiling had once been shiny and bright, but over the years had turned sepia from the nicotine. The sawdust floor was usually littered with crawfish shells and watermelon rinds, and in addition to the hot dogs and Vienna sausages and rat cheese and crackers and regular sausages, Sarge Jennings dispensed an appetizer of ground hot peppers, ketchup, and white vinegar called "Bottled Hell," which he claimed encouraged the beer trade and also the pungent Middle Eastern dish kibbi, since the store had once been owned by a Lebanese man named Skinny Hassan before the Crenshaws bought it in '46.

A substantial hand-painted sign on the interior wall said, "We reserve the right to refuse service to anyone, colored or white,: and a smaller one enigmatically declared, "Never Get Naked with Yankees," and another, "In God we trust, all others pay cash."

Another of the old veterans' favorite hangouts was Firehouse Number One, because Roach Weems was a fireman and always had a ball game on the radio, and, since it was adjacent to the jail, they could come out onto the lawn between poker hands and talk to the prisoners looking down from behind the barred windows upstairs. They also gathered at Son Graham's grocery next to his big unpainted house, the yard an indecipherable chaos of junk and outmoded equipment, with a narrow pathway leading through this uncommon debris to the cows and chickens and hogs in back. I had often come here as a boy to make childhood purchases, to be greeted effusively and by name, and to witness their raucous saturnalias. They kept their whiskey in a two-gallon jar marked "Vinegar," with other brands hidden behind the cornflakes, mayonnaise, and pickles. A great red rooster from Son Graham's backyard often perched high in the rafters.

When I was eleven, one stormy September afternoon at the tail end of a hurricane that had risen from the gulf, I sat enthralled in these unseemly quarters as they talked of French women and the goings-on at World War I camps. One of them claimed to have known Alvin York and talked about "Alvin" as if they had been intimate companions.

As the vinegar flowed, his takes about Sergeant York grew more and more inconsistent, conflicting with one another so direly that I began listening less for the facts and more for the contradiction. Then they broke into "Over There," and when they reached "the Yanks are coming," they were so loud and discordant that the rooster swooped down in a flurry of red feathers.

I recalled all these things as we bumped toward Locust Grove that afternoon, the Legionnaires as solemn and quiet as I had ever seen them.

The Locust Grove Baptist Church was more than a century old even then: a tall inverted V-shaped white exterior, high narrow windows with lime green shutters, a sloping whitewashed tin roof. The dust-mottled trees crept up to it on all sides and gave it the aspect of having been wrestled out of the hardwood forest itself which, of course, it had been. Towering on a hill, it dominated the hard, unyielding countryside. The sign over its high arched doorway said: "I am the Eternal Truth that endures from generation to generation."

We had forty-five minutes until the ceremony, and Arch and I went inside, under the high ceilings where it was cooler.

I sat down in one of the ancient handmade pews and looked up at the simple stained-glass windows and the slave gallery with its separate railed entrance and tried, as I had on that first day among the stones of the town cemetery, to steady my churning anxiety.

Arch was smiling royally as he wandered about. I took out the mouthpiece of my trumpet and started buzzing into it.

The Legionnaires had sprawled in the shade of an oak at the entrance to the graveyard. A hand-painted sign nailed to a tree by the gate said: "No Tres. From Dusk to Dawn." Luke and Woodrow and two gravediggers from the area were sitting in funeral home chairs next to the open grave under the Ricks canopy. The tombstones were stained with years of soil, and the snarled underbrush encroached upon the graves.

"Whites and colored are buried all in here," Woodrow was telling Luke. "Back in that brush you won't find nothin' but slaves. I wish they'd clear it out. All around in here, just like in town, you dig into old iron coffins. You just bury on top or move 'em over. This soldier today," Woodrow said, "he'll be buried on top of a little baby, but he won't know the difference."

"In France, you know," Luke said, with a kind of grudging reluctance as if he did not want to tell, but did, "when they buried out, they'd find bones all the time from World War I, unidentified bones."

"Bones is everywhere," Woodrow said, and shook his head. "I don't believe in ghosts, but they're there. The world's travelin' too fast. People don't listen no more to ghosts. *Bones everywhere*. Everywhere," the gravedigger repeated, and shook his head lugubriously too.

This was not exactly the kind of talk I needed. Wearing a dark suit and stiff shirt, I was beginning to feel a little weak in this stupefying atmosphere. I wandered away. A short-lived breeze tossed up a combination of dust and heat waves. A rabbit bounded out from behind a sassafras and scurried into the thicket. Wicked yellow jackets were everywhere and big buzzing horseflies, little swirling gnats, and black lizards with off-white stripes. This end of the county was cusp country for the Spanish moss, its northernmost locale, we were told in Coach Thomas's forestry class, and it hung from the older trees in iron gray pendants like silken threads.

At the edge of a flowering crape myrtle I came upon the

grave of a little girl. Her name was Angel Sweeney, and she had lived from March 2, 1870 to June 25, 1876. This too was June 25. She had died on this very day! No other Sweeneys were buried around her, and there she was, in a far corner of that backwoods graveyard, so forlorn and alone and long forgotten that I suddenly felt a great melancholy sorrow for little Angel — almost as much for her as I did for myself.

"Let's get ready!" Luke shouted just then.

The Legionnaires congregated at the grave. Woodrow and the gravediggers retired to the rear lawn of the church. Luke went with Arch to inspect his post in a stand of trees fifty yards away. In minutes came the procession.

They were country farmers who knew mortgage and setback and tenancy and scraggly cotton. As I stood there at attention, they surrounded the grave — men, women, and children, in an earnest proprietary silence. A uniformed military man, the escort, was on crutches and labored up the hill with Potter Ricks; all the toes on one foot had been blown off, we had been told, and I saw that one of his ears was gone. The father was tall and skinny, his face and knuckles sunburned, and his hair was plastered down with sweet-smelling tonic. There were two daughters, about ten and twelve. The mother was near collapse.

The preacher spoke of heroism and sacrifice and the ways of God. Big tears kept rolling down the father's face, which otherwise was without expression, and the younger daughter suddenly shrieked: "*Jimmy! Jimmy! Where are you?*" The elder girl was convulsed with weeping, her torso racked in trembling spasms. She fell to her knees in front of her chair, and Potter Ricks tried to help her up. Throughout all this, the mother repeated: "*Why, why, why, why?*"

And then a terrible thing happened. As the preacher recited the Lord's Prayer, and the silvery coffin slowly descended into the dark maw of the grave, the mother stood full height and screamed, a wail of insane and awful anguish, strode the few steps to the grave, and threw herself down into it! Arms reached out for her, but she sprawled facedown halfway inside, her undergarments and naked thighs exposed, and fought madly as Potter Ricks and the father together lifted her out.

After the guns were fired and I had played my equivocal notes and Arch his flawless response, the crippled escort presented the folded flag to the mother, who held him about the waist as he stood before her. The Legionnaires stacked their rifles and went to the family with great dignity and feeling, telling them that their son had died for his country and would always be remembered by everyone and that they were there representing the president of the United States, who could not make it to the funeral because he was so busy with the war.

The father's tears stopped for a moment, and the mother swayed back limp into her chair. Then Luke came over and knelt in front of them, holding the mother's hand in his, and then the daughters' and father's, and whispered to them for a long time. When the moment care for the family to leave, in an imperceptible wave the crowd parted to let them through, and they walked to the funeral car with a kind of doleful pride.

After they had finally disappeared in a veil of dust down the road, many of the others remained. There was a baffled rage among them that I had not seen before. *"Who's killin' our boys?"* one of them shouted. And another: "Let's drop the A-bomb!" They milled about for a while, as if the grave itself was their one magnetic touch with reality, and Luke and the Legionnaires went out and calmed them down, and slowly led them to their vehicles.

"That's the worst 'Taps' I ever heard, for Chrissake," Arch said to me when he came down out of the trees.

The graveyard was deserted now except for the usual retinue. Woodrow had the hood to the hearse open and was pouring water into the engine. Luke and Potter Ricks reclined listlessly in chairs. We sat down next to them. I was drenched with sweat, it was even dripping out of my ears and nose. When I had played my notes, there was so much moisture in my eyes that I had to close them to get through. Now I felt dehydration in the soul. I took off my coat and rolled up my sleeves.

Luke handed me his bandanna. "You look terrible."

"So do you." And he did. The skin around his eyes was deeply crinkled; his shoulders sagged wearily, and the sweat stains made half-moons around his armpits.

Plop. Plop. Plop. The gravediggers were at work behind us.

"It was bad," Luke said.

"It was bad," Potter assented.

"I guess we did all we could," Luke said.

"I've seen worse," Potter said.

"*Worse?*" I had to ask.

He was rubbing his glasses with his handkerchief. Exposd in the piercing sunlight, his eyes were pale and flaccid, like an old man's. "Double funerals. Triple funerals. Little children from car wrecks. Yes." He looked out ascetically across the stones, and suddenly there was such a swift, deadening pain in his features, an instant of dire and secret distress, as might have come with the sharp jab of a needle, that I was almost paralyzed by the sight. It vanished as quickly as it had come. Did he sense I had noticed? He briskly got up to talk with Woodrow at the hearse.

"Look at them," Luke said. "The old renegades deserve it."

Down by our station wagon, near the church, the Legionnaires had propped their carbines against the fenders. They were in their shirtsleeves passing around a bottle, then another. Immediately after the burial they had been quiet, almost sullen, perhaps even a little angry. Now they were taking copious gulps and talking spiritedly among themselves. I was beginning to learn that they were not really clerks or storekeepers or car salesmen or farmers, but honorably retired warriors.

And on the long drive back to town in our station wagon, I acknowledged this more fully. Their bantering desultory talk as they shared the bottles of Four Roses and I. W. Harper helped take my thoughts from the grave, at least for a while. As we pulled away from the church, Wash Rose handed one of the bottles to Arch and me in the back seat with his three fingers.

"Here, fellas," he said, "take a little swing — just don't tell your mamas."

The raw acrid taste of my first whiskey caused me to shudder, and I stifled a gag. In seconds I could feel a mellow warmth to my toes.

I described our vehicle as a station wagon, but that is not precisely correct. It was an old Pontiac sedan welded to the backside of a station wagon, so that it was really a makeshift omnibus with five rows of seats. The welding on the outside resembled scabrous scar tissue.

The owner of this unique vehicle was a crafty German merchant and loan shark named Herman von Schulte, or that is what he wished to be called (he was sometimes referred as the "Kraut"), who had actually fought against these very Legionnaires in 1918 and then migrated through New Orleans to the town in the 1920s, for what reason it had never been ascertained.

The black people regarded him as an enigma and thought him dangerous, and the Legion veterans treated him with a kind of buoyant and regal contumely. He was by any calculus the Silas Marner of Fisk's Landing. I had often observed this auslander with his soiled attire and obese midriff in the dual-countered drugstore trying to be friends with the old warriors who once were his foes or approaching them in his ceaseless perambulations up and down the main street with one of his feckless commercial propositions.

They ceaselessly taunted von Schulte about his aversion to the Jewish dry goods merchants whose establishments surrounded his, reminding him unmercifully that the town was blessed with a three-term Jewish mayor (vice president, too, of a mercantile store almost as large as Arch's father's and one of the owners of the wholesale grocery; and, for that matter, the owner of the cotton gin was Jewish, his grandfather having come up the river as the simplest and most peregrinating of peddlers, and when asked as an old man why he finally settled down permanently in Fisk's Landing was said to have replied that his horse died there, and then he started one of the most profitable junkyards in the whole of the flatland from there to Memphis).

In the name of honor, however, or whatever it was, the Legion men protected this garrulous and alien boulevardier from the more extreme of the home-front zealots during World War II, for after all he *was* technically an American citizen now, no matter how unlikely a one, and he had once even been a soldier as they had, although he *had* worn the kaiser's spiked helmet. But one suspects they told him, in the idiom, to watch his mouth. During that war he discovered he had a distant cousin in a German POW camp located farther north from us in the flatland, a corporal in the Afrika Korps, and when von Schulte visited him three or four times with cigarettes and candy, Sarge Jennings took it upon himself to go along, to make sure, he said, that they did not incarcerate the Kraut, too.

Still at this very moment, as the odd Siamese twin of a conveyance bounced and shifted on the gravel like a troubled ocean liner, Sarge Jennings was shouting: "The Kraut uses this to go get his interest payments from the piss-poor niggers. Charges forty percent and says he don't break even." To which Roach Weems amended: "Even the niggers don't think he's white!" And Fabian Tubbs: "The Kraut wouldn't be caught dead at the funerals — he's scared we'll aim the guns at *him*!"

In the moment Fabian Tubbs shouted this, we came onto the asphalt county road with the little Holy Roller church at the side, and the sudden stillness after the jolting gravel, this and surely the reference to the funeral, cast a quick and uneasy silence upon our band. It was getting on to twilight, and restless glints of heat lightning momentarily brightened the sky. The trees and Queen Anne's lace along the road were cloaked in dust, and the mingling sachet of honeysuckle and wild summer grasses filled the dusk like lusty perfume, so heavy that you could almost reach out and hold it in your hand. I knew then that nothing I might do, absolutely nothing, could ever obliterate from my memory the mother and daughters at the grave. I knew the thoughts of the men were there, too. I wondered what Georgia was doing. So often when I was in this masculine company, I thought of her, my antenna of love and feeling and fear.

After a time one of them asked Luke, "When's the next one?"

"Don't know."

Silence again. Then Sarge Jennings spoke in soft monologue, as if to foil the hush, more to himself it seemed than to the rest of us: "Do you know I fired volleys for General Featherstone in '28? Just been made commander at West Point. Died of pneumonia. His mother died of a broken heart in the bathtub the next day."

"That's the truth," Son Graham said. "I was at that funeral."

"Pershing came," Sarge Jennings said. "Right here to Fisk's Landing. Telegram from Coolidge. Monoplanes droppin' roses. Had a sergeant play 'Taps' that played for Woodrow Wilson. Did you know Featherstone was fuckin' MacArthur's first wife in the damned Ritz Hotel? She sent a dozen orchids to the funeral. Potter showed me the card."

He chuckled at the thought.

Everyone — men and boys — was thinking this over.

"That's the truth," Son Graham repeated, and chuckled proudly too. "It was common knowledge."

We had reached the final hill coming down, and the familiar green and white sign: "Fisk's Landing Corp. Limits: Pop. 10,184." Below us, the lights of the town were coming on.

"We can't let them little shits whip us like this," Roach Weems said.

* * *

149

Willie Morris (1934 – 1999) was born in Jackson, Mississippi, but his family later moved to Yazoo City, Mississippi. A Rhodes Scholar who studied at Oxford University, he served as the editor of the *Texas Observer* and then later as editor of *Harper's* magazine, becoming one of the most important editors in America during the turbulent Vietnam War and Civil Rights protest years. Eventually, he returned to Mississippi to become writer-in-residence at the University of Mississippi. He wrote two novels and numerous non-fiction books, including *North toward Home, Yazoo: Integration in a Deep-Southern Town, My Dog Skip* and *My Mississippi*, with photographs by his son David Rae Morris.

Shelby Foote in Paris / photo by his son, Huger Foote

SHOTS IN THE DARK

BY SHELBY FOOTE

For all its intensity, however, the talk of what had happened on Lamar Street would have been even more fervid if it has not had to share the limelight with another outrage of which the news, concerning Harley Drew and Amy and Jeff Carruthers, reached Bristol that same morning, two or three hours earlier, from Briartree down on Lake Jordan. There was less conjecture here but that was because people believed there was less room, or at any rate occasion, for conjecture.

The event, though far less common than in the old days — when, as they said, men were men — was not uncommon; indeed it was fairly cut-and-dried, though not without the tinge of humor that usually accompanies such bloodshed.

"Why, yes, of course," they told each other, speaking with the irrefutable positiveness which seems at times to be in direct ratio to the extent of error. For they were wrong. They were utterly and ironically wrong.

In the year following that first tourist court assignation, Amy's charm had continued to grow for Drew. He was not only fascinated by her person, he was fascinated by the things that surrounded her person — her clothes, her hair-style, even her cosmetics. He would wake in the night, switch on the bed lamp, and watch her sleeping beside him in the rented room, twenty to fifty miles from Bristol, depending on what point of the compass they had struck out this time.

Admiring the texture of her skin, he compared her to those other women, hotel girls like that first Alma ten years back, who had kept the peasant ankles and heavy thighs their forebears brought over from the old world: whereas with Amy, though the blood was basically peasant too, it had thinned to a sort of ichor, actually blue where the veins were near the surface. Cut her, she'd bleed blue, Drew told himself.

Or he would cross to the dresser where her overnight bag sat with the lid still raised, a patented model with compartments for everything; he would take out the urn-shaped jars and fluted bottles, unscrew the caps or ease out the glass stoppers, and smell them, the perfumed grease and distillations from the sperm whale, thinking: Ahhh. Then he would lift out the hand-stitched underwear, the pants and slips and petticoats with intricate unreadable monograms, unfolding and refolding them, feeling the whisper of silk against his palms, and to him they felt of money.

At last he would return to the bed and sit looking down at her. Even her sunburn represented money, its smooth tan consistency reminding him of the leisure that enabled her to acquire it.

He liked the way she smelled, duplicating what was in the various jars and bottles, and the fact that this fragrance could be bought (at as high as fifty dollars an ounce) made it no less enjoyable, no less heady — indeed, that was the pleasure. Fifty dollars a whiff! He thought, and his breath would quicken as he thought it. The fact was, he respected her enormously. It amounted to love, or very nearly love (a relative emotion anyhow, varying from person to person: Romeo and Mercutio for instance) or as near love, at any rate, as Drew was ever to come.

So it went. He had what he had prayed for, and the tick marks on the calendar, scoring their meetings, were for him what a mounting column of figures would be for a miser. Yet this success — like most successes, no matter how much longed for — bred only further desires, more distant goals. The Memphis and New Orleans visits had not been spent at the Peabody or the St. Charles or the Roosevelt; they had not dined at Galatoite's or Antoines. They had had to keep to the back streets, the remoter purlieus dodging recognition. Apparently this was all right with Amy, who had had her share of highlife in her time. But it was not all right with Drew; the memory of that three-year 'look around' was beginning to dim. If originally his desire had been to get her alone, now he wanted her at his side in public. He wanted to wear her like a badge, a panache, her and her expensive clothes, her careless, moneyed manner.

"Look at what *he's* got; look at that," he wanted to hear them murmur as he entered hotel lobbies and restaurants with Amy on his arm — hotels and restaurants barred to them now because of the dictates of prudence. Not that he was opposed to prudence: he, in fact, was the one who insisted on it. What Drew was opposed to was the necessity for prudence.

He had decided on his goal: his final goal, he told himself, incurably optimistic, still not having learned (and never *to* learn) that his desires were merely steps on an endless staircase leading nowhere. Divorce was no answer; the money was Jeff's. The answer lay in another direction, one that he was waiting for the courage — or anyhow the opportunity — to propose to Amy. He saw himself master of Briartree and all that went with it, including Amy as chatelaine. As for the present master, who would be surprised to hear that the houseboy, coming to work one morning, had found his employer crumpled at the foot of a flight of stairs, dead of a broken neck since late the night before?

Once this thought was in his mind, he would have been hard put to say when it had first occurred to him; it seemed so inescapably the only solution, he came to believe that he must have intended it from the start — as indeed perhaps he had, unconsciously. Yet even now, with it so firmly decided on as the answer to his problems, the only means of fulfilling his desires, he delayed proposing it to Amy: not because he had any fear of moral indignation on her part (he knew her far too well by now to expect any such reaction) but because he was afraid to add a questionable element to their union. He was enjoying himself, and one of his points of superiority over other men — call it that — was that he knew better than to tamper with happiness, a reflex most men find it impossible to abstain from. Whether or not she would agree was another matter, for at times she seemed inordinately fond of Jeff, not from love, of course, or even friendship, but rather from amusement. It was strange.

However, two events brought him to the point of a decision. For one thing, he was offered a job with a Memphis bank, a really exceptional position, and though he did not exactly decline it — he never exactly declined any offer, as has been said — he did not accept it. To his considerable surprise he found that he was not even tempted to accept it. He could not have left Amy if he had wanted to.

Thus he discovered that he had lost his freedom, which had been the one thing he thought of himself as prizing highest. The Barcroft business, as he now termed his long engagement to Amanda, had been a different matter: he had felt all along that he could break it off whenever he chose, which in fact was what he had done. But now he thought of himself as a man tied down, and that was bitter.

The other was not really a single event; it was a series of them, more or less alike, modeled after the first one back in July of the previous year when the new bridge over the river was opened to traffic and they went across to Arkansas for a night. They had checked in at a tourist court and were driving along the highway in search of a restaurant, when they saw HANNAHS spelled in lights.

"Hey: a nightclub!" Amy cried.

Drew turned in, though not without misgivings. The entrance was around at the side, two steps leading up to a closed door, beyond which they heard music and stamping feet. When Drew opened the door it was like looking into a cage of lions and monkeys at feeding time, arms and legs blurred with motion, bodies spinning furiously, skirts flaring, trouser legs flopping. This was the jitterbug, which they had heard of but had never seen before. To them it was reminiscent of the Twenties, like the Charleston gone insane.

A row of booths ran down each side of the room. At the far end a blue-and-gold nickelodeon with moving lights was turned up full, and at this end a long window was cut waist-high into the wall so that you looked over a counter into a room where beer and ice and chasers were kept, and even a pump-up stove for toasting sandwiches. A waitress, dressed no differently from the dancing women except that she wore about her waist a towel with a pocket sewed on it to hold her tips, kept moving between the booths and the counters, crying orders shrilly to be heard above the din. Drew and Amy found a booth in back, not far from the music, which beat against their eardrums.

"Oo! what a dive!" Amy cried happily, her voice as high-pitched as the waitress's. "Break out the bottle, honey lamb. Numb me afore I go deaf."

Her eyes had an excited glitter, as from fever, and she turned her head this way and that, watching the dancers and the drinkers.

"Look at that one," she kept saying; "Look at *that* one."

She even pointed, and sometimes the people would look back at her, scowling.

Drew's misgiving increased. He could see the headline now: BRISTOL BANKER INVOLVED IN ROADHOUSE BRAWL.

In the booth behind them, nearer the blare of the music, a man and his wife were arguing. Their voices came through during pauses when the machine was changing records.

"I never said I wasn't."

"Oh, *you*."

"Some fun, all right—"

"You think *I* like it?"

"You—"

"Ah, *you*!"

Then the new record would drown them out. But they came through each time the music paused.

"You—"

"Ah, *you*."

Marital bliss, Drew thought, refilling Amy's glass, which she slid across the table at him. That was when the first one came up—a mousy man with a receding chin and claret-colored suspenders.

"Say, mister," he said. "Mind if I dance a turn with your girl, if she's willing?"

"Thanks," Drew said. "Not yet awhile. But thanks."

Amy watched him walk away. "I *like* this place," she said over the rim of her glass. "I really do."

"A little too informal for me," Drew said.

Then another came up, more positive. "Dance your girl?"

"Sorry," Drew said, watching Amy. The man stood for a moment looking down at him, hard-faced in a damp blue shirt, the sleeves rolled right above his biceps. Drew still did not return his look and finally he shrugged and walked away.

"Not my type," Amy said, sliding her glass across the table. She had even sucked the ice dry.

"Come on," Drew said. "Let's get out of here."

"*Fill* it," she said.

He filled it. This was her third and he was still on his first.

"Hats more like it," she said presently.

He thought she meant the drink, but when he looked he saw that she was returning the stares of three men in a booth across the room. They were gabardine shirts wilt pearly buttons and contrasting yokes, skin-tight Levis bleached sky-blue, and cowboy boots.

"Makes me wish I worn my jodhpurs," Amy said.

Looking back across the room, Drew saw that one of the men had risen from the booth and was coming toward them. The tallest of the three, he had high cheekbones and a bleached space at the top of his forehead where he wore his hat.

"Dance this next?" he said, standing beside the table. He spoke directly to Amy.

"Be back honey," she said to Drew before he could decline. She was already standing,: had been standing, he realized, since the man first rose to cross the room.

"The name is Tex," Drew heard him say as he put his arm around her waist. He said it solemnly, as if he might have been saying he had a million dollars or tonight was the end of the world. They danced away and Drew was left nursing his drink.

In the course of the next three records he watched them through a haze of smoke and whirling couples. The man was teaching her the jitterbug, throwing her out and pulling her back, showing her how to truck with her knees held close together, pigeon-toed. The hard high heels of his boots made a clatter like hoofs. She seemed to be enjoying it, but in the interval between the third and fourth records — one of those sudden silences which seemed even louder, somehow, than the blare — she came back fanning herself, saying "Woo. Give me a drink. My God." Her upper lip was beaded with perspiration; her eyes were glassy. She drank.

"You see him?" she said. "Tex? My God. His hands were even busier than his feet."

"Stay away from him then."

"Well—" The fifth record had started by now.

"Dance?" they heard.

They looked up. It was Tex.

"She's not dancing," Drew said evenly.

"Not?" Tex said. "Ain't that kind of up to the lady?"

"It's up to me," Drew said, watching Amy. "It's up to me and I say she's not dancing."

By this time the two friends had crossed the floor; they stood one on each side of Tex, all three looking lean and capable in their cowboy clothes, a little taller than life in their high-heel boots. Amy looked at them, then back to Drew. The music stopped. Eyes glassy, she suddenly leaned forward, patted his and arm and spoke. It sounded loud against the silence.

"Go Drew boy. Pop him one."

BRISTOL BANKER INVOLVED IN ROADHOUSE BRAWL ran across his mind like a streamer, like a headline dummy across an editor's desk: whereupon he did a thing which, even as he did it, he knew he would never forget, would never remember except with a sense of shame. He looked up at the three men — they stood with their arms held slightly away from their sides, a look of almost happy anticipation on their faces — and smiled; he smiled broadly.

"Sit down fellows. Have a drink," he said. "Slide over Amy. Make room for our friends."

Yet behind the glibness and the smile there was an ache of shame; he had never declined a fight before. He thought of the moment he wished he had it here to show them.

They were a party. The whiskey was gone in less than half an hour — bonded stuff, of which the three men showed their appreciation by swishing it around in their mouths before they swallowed. All this time, speculative, bemused, Tex sat looking down the front of Amy's dress like a man on a high-dive platform contemplating a jackknife or a gainer. Drew kept as brave a face through this as he had through the loss of his whiskey. Amy, who had had more than her share of the bottle, got more and more glassy-eyed, until finally she went to sleep.

"Well—" Drew said. He rose. "Time to go."

The others helped him half guide, half carry her to the door and out to the car. When one of the her breasts tumbled out, Tex leaned forward and with a surprisingly delicate circumspection, of which Drew would never have suspected him capable, stuffed it back. Even then, however, Drew lacked the courage to refuse to shake hands with him. He shook hands all around, for he kept seeing that headline with a subhead: *Millionaires' Wife Was Bone of Contention in Fracas, Witnesses State.* As he drove off he saw the three of them in the rear-vision mirror, silhouetted against the electric sign. Bastards! He thought, and wiped his palm against his thigh.

This was only the first in a series of such incidents, for Amy had an increasing fondness for these places. When he cursed her proclivity for associating with truck drivers, imitation cowboys and roadhouse touts, however, he paused to consider that it also included small-town bank employees; he was forced to reconcile himself to her tastes. Yet as the incidents became more frequent he saw clearly that marriage was the only answer. Then if they went to such places and she said, "Go on, Drew boy. Pop him one," he would pop him one with pleasure. BRISTOL BANKER DEFENDS WIFE was a headline he cold stomach and be proud of.

Then in September, soon after the war got under way in Europe, he received the offer from the Memphis bank, and having refused it he found his position intolerable being required not only to act the role of a physical coward (for which he was in no way suited) but also to turn down all outside advantages, no matter how exceptional. It seemed to him that he was putting so much more into this thing than she was—in spite of the fact that she would stuff bills of rather large denominations into his side coat pocket as they drove out of town; for what was that but money? While he was giving his peace of mind, his self-respect, his future.

A burning sense of the injustice of all this brought him at

last to the proposal of murder. The week he received the offer from Memphis he and Amy were driving out of town on a Saturday morning; it had been a year and seven months since the night in the state-line tourist court.

"What I don't like is all this waiting," he said, hardly knowing how to begin, in spite of all the thinking he had done. Mainly he was exasperated but he was also a little afraid; for you could never tell about women. They had stopped at a traffic signal and he fiddled with the steering wheel spokes while waiting for the light to change. "Damn it Amy — "

* * *

He paused, then said it again.

"Damn it, Amy — "

But she was scarcely listening. She had this ability to blank out when the talk grew serious, just as some people can do when a radio program is held up for the commercial. Sunlight fell in long gold penciling through the leaves of the oaks and sycamores that grew between the sidewalk and the curb; now was the climax of summer and the nights were perceptibly longer, though no cooler. Maybe the guns in Europe would bring rain — that was how they had explained the rain she remembered falling ceaselessly through her early teens, the long Carolina afternoons with a patter on the windowpanes and the nights when there was a steady drumming on the roof; "It's the guns in Europe," they told her, and now the guns were barking and growling again. A woman dressed in gray stood at the curb, holding a market basket with both hands. The light was with her but she did not move. Then it changed, glared green, and Drew engaged the clutch; the car rolled forward.

He was silent for a time, apparently having decided that 'Damn it Amy' was the wrong approach. They were well out of town before he spoke again, telling her — to her surprise, for he seldom spoke of the war — a rather tiring story about a man, a friend of his, who got gas in his eyes. Lewsite, he said. It was not very interesting; she was looking out over the fields, alternately green or green-and-white, depending on whether the pickers had passed over them; she only heard snatches of the story. Presently the scene was a hospital behind the lines, the friend in bed with a bandage over his eyes, and Drew was sitting beside him. They were talking; the man was asking for something. He was blind and they were about to send him home. A pistol.

"Did you give it to him?" Amy said, interrupting.

"I did."

"Wasn't that kind of risky?"

"Risky? How, risky?"

"The pistol: they'd trace it."

"Mm—no. It wasn't mine. It was one I picked up in a retreat."

He kept his eyes on the road, and suddenly for no good reason Amy knew that it was all a lie. He was making it up.

"Did he use it?"

"He used it; he used it that night." Drew kept his eyes on the road. He drove for a while, saying nothing. Then he said, "Do you think I did right?"

"I guess. If that's what he wanted."

"No: I mean apart from that. He was sort of delirious anyhow—off his rocker. I mean because of the blindness. Wasn't he better off?"

"I don't know. It depends on how he felt about it. Look at Jeff."

Drew said nothing to this, but he began to glance at her from time to time, barely turning his head. She wondered why he had gone to the trouble of making all this up, this rigmarole about a blind man and a pistol, and suddenly she remembered something Jeff had said five years ago: *You're all the way evil, Amy.* She smiled. 'I'm going to take a little nap,' she intended to say, but she was asleep before she could form the words.

Then he woke her. They were there. The sun was coming straight down. It was noon "I was sleeping so good," she said. "I dreamed—I dreamed—"But she could not remember; she gave it up. "Where are we?"

"That's Clarksdale down the road a piece."

He had already checked in at the office. They went into the cabin It was neater and cleaner than most; there were dotted Swiss curtains at the windows and a reading lamp on each of the twin beds—they had reached the twin-beds stage by now. Amy looked around. "Why, this is downright *nice*. What's our name?"

"Amos Tooth," he said solemnly.

They both laughed, for this was a game they played; Drew signed a different name on the register each trip. He was really quite ingenious in this respect. Once he had signed 'Major Malcolm Barcroft,' which wasn't very funny—being a sort of private joke—but he made up for it next time by signing 'David Copperfield.' Amy was always '& wife.' After the first few times he began to call her that. "Shall we go eat, & Wife?"

There was a restaurant just up the road. They ate and came straight back to bed. Later the afternoon sun beat golden against the shades, which billowed and sighed from time to time when there was a little breeze. Languid, Amy lay and listened; the stick at the bottom of the shade made a tapping against the sill; the rhythm of it put her to sleep, and when she woke darkness had almost come.

Drew lay in the adjoining bed, a pale naked shadow blowing smoke rings that were steel-gray in the gloom. She watched him through the lattice of her lashes. After a while she said, "Why'd you make up all that business about the blind man?"

"Make up?"

"Yes."

He paused. Caught unprepared he was never a very good liar. "I wanted to see how you felt," he said, and added immediately: "Besides, it really did happen, to a friend of mine."

"The blind man?"

"No, the one who gave him the pistol."

"Oh. Did he really give it to him?"

"Well—he started to. And afterwards he wondered if he shouldn't have."

"I see." She thought a while. "What happened to him?"

"The blind man? I don't know. Somebody said he really did kill himself, on the boat going back. I don't know. There were lots like him."

She watched him light another cigarette, his face dead white in the flare. When he blew out the match the darkness was complete; it was as if night had fallen during that brief spurt of flame. He lay back, the cigarette tip glowing and fading like a signal light.

"Were you very scared in the war?" she asked.

"Not very. No. I was what you might call moderately scared. Comparatively speaking, that is." He spoke slowly. "Looking back on it—the excitement and all—I guess it was maybe the best time of my life. I know an old man lives on Lamar Street would sell his soul for ten minutes of what I had almost two years of."

Amy let this pass. The cigarette glowed and faded, glowed and faded. He was thinking. Then he said, "We've all got about the same amount of courage. The difference comes in whether were willing to use it, provided we get a chance. Take you and me. We want something beyond all this" —he made a gesture, describing a red arc with the tip of his cigarette" —but whether we take it or not is up to us. It's a question of using courage."

"What do you mean?"

"This," he said, and the springs creaked under him. He sat up, flipping the cigarette through the bathroom door. It fell like a miniature comet with a little burst of sparks against the tiles. While he talked it faded and presently it went out. This is what he had been working toward. He took his time; he made it clear. Who would be surprised to hear that the houseboy coming to work one morning had found the blind man crumpled at the foot of the stairs, dead of a broken neck since sometime late the night before? They'd say he got up for a drink of water or a midnight snack and missed his footing; it was just that simple.

Drew spoke in a conspirator's undertone — not so much in fear of being overheard however, as in an attempt to gauge her reaction to the words. When he had finished he waited for her to speak. She waited too. It was almost a full minute before she replied.

"You want me to hold his legs or something while you trip him?"

In the dark he could not see that she was smiling her slow, down-tending smile; he did not hear the mockery in her voice. He was too delighted with the words themselves to pay much attention to the tone in which they were spoken.

"No, no," he said, leaning forward, speaking rapidly; "all I want is —"and was interrupted by a burst of laughter. While she laughed he sat here in the darkness hating her. It was some little time before she could speak, though not as long as it seemed. Then she said:

"I swear, Drew boy; I swear you take the cake."

This came just in time; for the truth was, she was beginning to weary of him, and not only of him but of the Delta too. Not that he had failed her in the prime respect: the days of what he, in his artilleryman's jargon, called "muzzle bursts" were long since past, and she had frequent cause to bless her patience through the trying first few weeks: nowadays in their gladiatorial contests it was quite often Amy who lay sweat-drenched and exhausted, spread-eagle on the mat, and Drew who leaned above her, hawk-faced and triumphant, glaring down — "There! There, by God!" — victorious after the bitter defeats of the early encounters. She had no complaint in that direction. Paradoxically, what was wearying her of him was what had drawn her in the first place: her essential promiscuity. It was really that simple. She wanted a change.

A year and six months was a very long time, longer than she had been involved with Jeff — in this particular sense. What kept it going was the clandestine excitement, the conspiratorial air, and the various subterfuges Drew employed. She had been right about the conspiratorial air from the first, and now it turned out that he had been right to adopt it. For that was what held her, that and his skill at subterfuge; he took no chances even with a blind man.

Watching his grave demeanor at the Briartree dinner table while he discussed finances or the world political situation with Jeff and turned to her from time to time with the deference any guest owes any hostess; "Isn't that so, Mrs. Carruthers?" (or, later: "Isn't that so, Amy?" since he decided that too much formality was itself suspicious) was better than watching a movie. He should have been an actor, she decided. Sometimes she would laugh till tears of mirth stood in her eyes; she had to cover her face with a napkin and pretend to be choking.

"Take some water," Drew would say solicitous; he never so much as smiled at such a time. The most he permitted himself was a twinkle deep in the pupil of each eye, and that would set her to laughing all the harder, until finally she would have to leave the table. All this, together with the series of names on hotel and tourist court registers, from David Copperfield to Amos Tooth--& Wife — appealed enormously to her simple and somewhat cruel sense of humor.

Some nights when they were stopping only twenty or thirty miles away, Drew would leave her soon after dark and return about three hours later. He would wake her and sit beside her on the bed and tell how he had sat talking with Jeff at Briartree throwing him off the scent; for otherwise he might have begun to wonder at never seeing Drew when Amy was away, and from there it would be an easy step to assuming that they were together.

"Where's Amy?" I asked, and he said – you know how he talks: "Oh she's off to Memphis shopping. She's buying an awful lot of clothes here lately, seems to me."

Drew imitated Jeff's voice to perfection, querulous and trembly in the upper registers; he even managed to look a good deal like him when he was quoting, puffing out his cheeks a bit, drawing in the corners of his mouth, and letting his eyes come unfocused. Amy had to laugh. He should indeed have been an actor, she decided.

Even so, there was a limit to how long she could be amused in such a fashion. The jokes were not so funny the third or fourth time around; she wanted a new pair of hands moving nervously over her person, a new voice panting different words in her ear. She had begun to think of a break.

This excursion to the Delta—the blind seed swimming home—had long since served whatever vague purpose she had had in mind.(What was his name? Perkins. Was that his name?) She was bored, almost to the point of doing something about it. Then in the quiet September twilight Drew proposed the murder and her interest was revived.

"You want me to hold his legs?" she said. She had underestimated him, and even though she laughed there was admiration behind the laughter. Besides, she soon stopped laughing.

She had known from the start what he was really after, beyond the flesh, and it seemed to her now that she should have expected this. From the night of their first intimacy Drew had listened with great interest when she told of her experiences in the world of highlife, especially during the five-year European celebration of the inheritance. He listened, absorbed, while she told of Jeff shooting at the patter of the widow's little Spaniard's pumps; then he roared with laughter, slapping his thigh.

But this was unusual. Mostly he listened with quiet pleasure and anticipation, like a child being introduced to history through tales of kings and heroes, for he looked forward to doing such things himself — with Jeff's money and Jeff's wife. So she might have expected the proposal, she realized soon after he had made it, and she stopped laughing. For here was an excitement for amusement beyond anything she had imagined.

Not that she had intentions of going through with it. Jeff suited her too well in too many ways, and she had few delusions as to Drew in the role of husband. What was more, she knew the boredom would return, and later the break. But she saw possibilities for an amusing interim and she worked it for all it was worth, believing that she was in command of the situation. This was the beginning of a more intimate relationship among the three of them — a sort of rehearsal, as Drew believed, for what was to come.

Soon after the first of the year, he and Amy no longer went afield for their pleasures; they took them right there in the house approximately under the blind man's nose. Drew was not entirely without caution, remembering the potshots at the Spaniard but he came to believe that he would more or less welcome such a scene. For a small risk, even though no plea would be needed before the world — let alone the coroner's jury, whose verdict, if one were called for, would be Accidental Death — it would give him a chance to plead self-defense to his conscience.

This moved swiftly. Amy could sense an approaching climax. Apparently Drew could sense it too, for now their love encounters had the frantic jerkiness of such scenes in the old time motion pictures (in the course of which the audience, crouched beneath the lancing beam, kept expecting Valentino or John Gilbert, stigmatized in flickering black and white, to look up from his work and cry with hot impatience — it was part of the illusion — 'Get those cameras out of here!'); yet nothing happened.

Then one April night they tried something new. Drew had dinner at Briartree and afterwards the three of them were sitting in the living room. The electric clock hummed on the mantelpiece. For a long time nobody said anything. The servants had left. Then Drew said, "Well" — rising; it was barely after nine — "thanks for the meal. I'd better be heading back."

"Early yet," Jeff told him.

"Hard day tomorrow," Drew said; "Good night," and Amy went to see him out, something she had never done in the old days. "Night," he said, opening the door.

"Good night," she said, and she reached across in front of him and slammed it. They stood together in the hall, facing the closed door. He did not understand until she pointed to the stairs. Then, obediently, he tiptoed up and waited on the landing while she went into the living room; "Good night," he heard her say to Jeff. She joined him on the stairs and they went quietly to her room.

After a while they heard Jeff paying the phonograph. He played it until midnight; then they heard him come upstairs and go down the hall to his room. Drew left just before dawn, arriving at Mrs. Pentecost's with plenty of time for a bath and a shave before breakfast.

"Hard day tomorrow," he had said, not meaning it; but it was. He was red-eyed numb with the need for sleep. You're not as young as you used to be, he thought. However, he reminded himself that the time was near when he would be delivered. He was upstairs now, familiar with the floor plan; this was all a sort of rehearsal, a dry run, and he continued to labor at it.

Twice again in the next two weeks he said good night and stayed, coming to work red-eyed the following day. The fourth time was the second Monday in May and the papers were full of the German break-through; von Rundstedt had crossed the Meuse. After dinner Drew and Jeff and Amy sat in the living room. It was all as before. The clock hummed; the servants had left; nobody said anything. Then Drew rose.

"Well. Thanks again. I guess I'd better be going."

"So early?" Jeff said.

"Rough day tomorrow," Drew told him, knowing it was true. Except for this knowledge it was all as before. He and

Amy rose. But now Jeff rose too, and the three of them crossed to the entrance hall, where Drew took his hat from the refectory table. Amy went to the front door with him but Jeff stopped in the doorway of the study; he would play some records before bedtime. Drew opened the door. "Night," he said. Jeff raised one hand, waving as if from a distance though he was only fifteen feet away.

"Good night," Amy said, wondering what Drew would do. She had only an instant to wonder, for he slammed the door and they both turned together, watching Jeff. It seemed to Amy that he must hear their heartbeats He continued to stand in the study doorway and his eyes were fixed on Drew; there was an illusion that his eyesight had returned. Then, as if to reinforce the illusion, he said in a sudden but level voice, still as if looking at Drew: "Who do you think you're fooling?"

Drew was so taken aback he almost answered. But Amy stepped in front of him, walking toward her husband. "Why should I try to fool you? I haven't fooled you yet."

"That I know of, you mean."

"Maybe that's what I do mean. Yes. Good night."

Jeff shrugged and went into the study and Amy stopped at the foot of the stairs. There she turned and beckoned to Drew, who tiptoed past the study door, feel silent on the carpet. As he went by he saw the blind man seated in his armchair, his face toward the hall. Again there was that illusion of recovered sight: Drew flinched. He and Amy went upstairs together.

When they were in the bedroom he said nervously, "You think he saw me?"

"*Saw* you?"

"Knew I was there."

"Oh, he makes all kinds of guesses and stabs in the dark. Here: unhook me."

Apparently she was right, for presently they heard the phonograph. It was Jelly Roll Morton's *Two Nineteen*. At first he talked. "The first blues I no doubt ever heard," he said. He talked some more, hands moving over the keys. Then he began to sing, and it was as if you could see him throw his head back, the drawn ascetic face of a high-yellow monk, the skin fitting close to the skull.

> *Two Nineteen done cared by baby away.*
> *Two Seventeen bring her back some day.*

* * *

But Drew was right: Jeff had 'seen' him — meaning he knew he was there. For some time now, since not long after New Year's, he had been increasingly aware of what was going on between them. What was more, he knew exactly where, for he had heard them go upstairs together the week before — Drew had come on from Guard drill, wearing his uniform, and Jeff had heard the creak of his boots and the tiny chink of his spur and saber chains.

This was early May; he had not gone to the door with them, and as he sat in the living room he heard the door slam, followed by the sound of what he thought at first was Amy coming down the hall alone. Then he remembered that she was wearing no bracelet, and thus he identified the faint jingling which no one but a blind man would have heard.

"I'm going up," she said from the hall; the chinking stopped.

"Good night," he said; it began again, combined now with the creak of boots moving up the stairs.

His first reaction was incredulity, then rage, then incredulity again: he simply could not believe his luck. For more than three months now, with increasing fervor as the conviction grew, he had been plotting, hoping for some move on their part which would place them at his disposal.

Now it was here. Yet he did nothing that night, remembering how the incidents involving the Austrian ski instructor and

Mama's Spaniard had ended in ridicule; this time he would move according to plan. Besides, this was a new kind of jealousy — double-barreled, so to speak, directed not only at the man but at Amy too, and therefore requiring double caution. She was the alienor and Drew the loved one. Thus on one hand; on the other, she was the property and Drew the thief. On both counts action was required.

Yet he did nothing that night. He went into the study and planned his campaign. Later he went up to his room, put on pajamas, and lay in bed, completing the details. Then he got up and rehearsed it, moving quietly down the hall to the door of Amy's room; he could hear them speaking in whispers. He stayed there for perhaps ten minutes, his ear against the panel. At last he came back to his room. He lay smiling in the moonlight. Finally he fell asleep, still smiling, and woke with sunlight warm on his face; he had not heard Drew leave. But that was all right — Drew's leaving had no part in the campaign.

So ten days later, the second Monday in May, he was ready; so ready in fact, so much in the advantage that he could afford to be sporting about it, like a hunter letting a duck rise off the water. He followed them into the hall and stood at the doorway of the study.

"Who do you think you're fooling," he said when the front door slammed, speaking directly to Drew, eyes fixed on the place where he knew he was standing. He heard him gasp and he felt the thrill that is the reward of sportsmanship, the hunter's consideration for the hunted. This was the greatest intimacy yet; it was like an embrace, flesh touching flesh; for a moment he experienced something akin to buck fever.

Then Amy came forward and spoiled it. Jeff replied angrily, going into the study, where presently he heard Drew tiptoe past, his footsteps like so many powder puffs dropped from a height.

He listened while they climbed the stairs, and that completed Phase One; he had planned it in three phases. Now began Phase Two, which would end when he reached the door of Amy's bedroom. He put the Jelly Roll Morton record on the phonograph, and when that was through he played another — any man to any woman in any dingy hotel room, the man abed, the woman with her hand on the knob of the door.

> *Don't leave me here.*
> *Don't leave me here.*
> *But if you just must go*
> *Leave a dime for beer.*

It was one of his favorites, yet he scarcely heard it. When it was through he wiped it with the complexion brush and put it back. Then he selected a Bessie Smith, and this time he listened in spite of himself.

> *I woke up this morning*
> *With an awful aching head,*
> *I woke up this morning*
> *With an awful aching head;*
> *My new man had left me*
> *Just a room and a empty bed.*

Her warm, proud voice soared on though Bessie herself had been dead over two years now. She died after an automobile accident fifty miles from Briartree; they got her to a hospital in time but the authorities couldn't let her in — her color wasn't right and she bled to death.

He listened, head bent, wearing crepe-soled shoes and white wool socks, gray flannel slacks and a polo shirt unbuttoned at the throat. This was a different Jeff from the one who arrived twelve years ago from Carolina or the one who returned from Europe less than five years back. His tan had faded; he had gone to fat. The pectoral muscles, formerly the hard square plates of an athlete, had sagged to almost womanish proportions; the ripple of ribs had disappeared beneath a fatty casing that thickened his torso from armpits to fundament.

More than anything he resembled a eunuch, or rather the classic conception of a eunuch — as if the knife-sharp sliver of windshield glass had performed a physical as well as a psychological castration.

Yet under that ruined exterior there still lurked, like a ghost in a ruined house, the halfback who had heard his name roared from the grandstand, who had welcomed the shocks, the possible fractures and bruises and concussions, for love (or hatred) of one among the mass of tossing pennants as at the tournaments of old, and who had won her — though not through the football prowess after all — so that now, nearly twenty years later, she waited upstairs, inviting him to another encounter, the chain of flesh relinked And now, as before, he welcomed the shocks, the fractures and concussions. He took out the pistol. It was where he had kept it ever since Switzerland, in the nest of wires under the used-needles tray, along with a box containing thirty-eight of the original fifty cartridges. Six were in the pistol; the other six had been fired in the Cannes hotel. He had not fired it since, though every few months he would strip and clean and oil it.

Once he had put the muzzle in his mouth to see what suicide was like, but there was such a compulsion to pull the trigger that he took it out in a hurry, badly frightened, and from then on his gorge would rise when he remembered the taste of oily metal. He thought of none of his now, however; he merely sat with the pistol in his lap, waiting for the record to end.

> *Lord, he's got that sweet something*
> *And I told my gal-friend Lou;*
> *He's got that sweet something*
> *And I told my gal-friend Lou.*
> *From the way she's raving*
> *She must have gone and tried it too*

That was the end of the first side of the record. Jeff was expecting it, waiting with his hand above the tone arm, so that when the final note was wailed he lifted the needle clear of the groove, flipped the record over, and let the tone arm down.

For three revolutions it gave a mechanical hissing. Then the music began again: Empty Bed, Part Two.

When my bed gets empty
Makes me feel awful mean and blue,
When my bed get empty
Makes me feel awful mean and blue,
My springs are getting rusty
Sleeping single like I do.

Bessie said 'blue' with the French *u* language students try so hard for. When she said it the first time Jeff was already at the foot of the stairs; when it came around again he was at the top, walking quietly on crepe soles down the hall, pistol in hand. He moved with the confidence of the blind at home, not having to pause for bearings, not even having to count his steps, but able at any given moment to reach out and touch whatever tables and chairs and doorknobs happened to be within reach, as if the objects and doorknobs happened to be within reach, as if the objects exerted some sort of aura, an emanation, or had a least a reflectiveness, twitching the invisible cat-whiskers of the blind.

He paused at Amy's bedroom door: Phase Three.

For all his careful planning, however, his rigid adherence to schedule, he was early. Leaning with his ear against the panel he heard the preliminary whispers still in progress, punctuated by the squeak of kisses. Downstairs Bessie sang the blues, indifferent to all misery but her own, and between the lines a trombone throbbed and moaned.

He give me a lesson
That I never had before,
He give me a lesson
That I never had before;
When he got through teaching me
From my elbows down was sore.

Charley Green was the trombone, he remembered. Then he froze, standing with his ear against the panel. Beyond the door the whispering had stopped; he heard the first tentative creaking of the springs. But still he waited, the pistol in his right hand and his left hand on the knob. Downstairs the song was into its final verse, in the course of which the tentative creak from the room beyond changed to a regular groaning, muffled, rhythmic, and profound. He turned the knob.

When you get good loving
Never go and spread the news;
Gals will double cross you
And leave you with them
Empty Bed Blues.

On the last note, just before the mechanical hissing began, Jeff opened the door, went in, and closed it quietly with a backward movement of his arm. The innerspring groaning was louder now, guiding him to the bed. Though he did not know it, a bedside lamp was burning; as he came nearer his shadow on the wall behind him loomed hunch-shouldered and gigantic. He moved quickly, silently.

Halting alongside the bed he placed his left hand in the small of Drew's back, palm down, rested the base of his other fist upon it, gripping the pistol, and walked the left hand up Drew's backbone like a tarantula. This was all according to plan; the backbone guided the pistol to the brain; this time he would not miss.

Drew, if he felt the hand at all, must have thought it was Amy's. However, it is unlikely that he felt it, for he was approaching that brief ecstasy which is characterized — as is no other sensation, except perhaps extreme pain (and maybe nausea) — by a profound indifference to the world around him; whatever feelings of warmth and tenderness may lap the shores of these tiny timeless islands in the time-stream, no man is ever more alone than in this moment of closest possible contact.

Amy, though, feeling something brush her knee, opened her eyes and saw Jeff with the pistol. She gave a yelp and a start of surprise. But here again, Drew, if he noticed at all, must have taken her cry of alarm and her sudden writhing as evidence of a gratification similar to his own. Yet it was no matter — he had so little time anyhow; for then Jeff pulled the trigger. He fired twice.

At the first show Drew merely jerked spasmodically, but at the second he gave a leap that raised him clear of the mattress. He fell back, tumbling sideways, and rolled to the floor at Jeff's feet. Meanwhile Amy, freed of his weight, scrambled out of bed in the other direction. Then she made her first mistake: she ran for the far corner instead of the door. Her bare feet made thudding sounds on the carpet and Jeff turned, coming toward her around the end of the bed.

Neither of them spoke. Amy crouched in the corner as if ashamed of her nakedness, watched him coming nearer; she had terror in her face. Jeff advanced with his arms outspread, like a man catching a turkey in a barn lot. The closer he came the less room there was left to go around him; the sooner she tried to reach the door, the better her chances were. She decided to make a rush for it, and that was when she made her second mistake; she went to the right, away from the hand that held the pistol. As it was, she almost made it; she was almost past when his free hand grazed her hair and suddenly clutched. He caught her.

"Jeff!" she cried, but he dragged her inexorably across his hip, his left hand still grasping her hair — they posed thus for an instant, motionless, like dancers performing a deadly Apache — and slashed at her twice with the pistol, once at her right cheek-bone and once across the bridge of her nose; then, chipping her teeth, he shoved the muzzle in her mouth. Downstairs the phonograph hissed and hissed.

There were four shots left.

* * *

"Shots in the Dark" is excerpted with permission from Shelby Foote's novel, *Love in a Dry Season*. Copyright © 1951 by Shelby Foote. Copyright renewed 1979 by Shelby Foote.

Shelby Foote (1916 – 2005) was born in Greenville, Mississippi, and died in Memphis, Tennessee, in between those years studying at the University of North Carolina and serving during World War II in the European theater as a captain of field artillery. Best known for his remarkable three-volume history of the Civil War, *The Civil War: A Narrative*, he began his writing career first as a newspaper reporter and then as a novelist. His other novels include *September, September, Shiloh: A Novel,* and *Follow Me Down*.

Ellen Douglas / Photo courtesy Ayres Haxton

ON THE LAKE

BY ELLEN DOUGLAS

Late summer in Philippi is a deadly time of year. Other parts of the United States are hot, it is true, but not like the lower Mississippi Valley. Here the shimmering heat — the thermometer standing day after day in the high nineties and the nights breathless and oppressive — is compounded, even in a drought, by the saturated air. Thunderheads piling up miles high in the afternoon sky, dwarf the great jet planes that fly through them. The air is heavy with moisture, but for weeks in July and August there is no rain.

In July, Lake Okatukla begins to fall. The lake, named from a meandering bayou that flows into it on the Arkansas side, bounds the town of Philippi on the west. It was once a horse-shoe-shaped bend of the Mississippi, but its northern arm is blocked off from the river now by the Nine-Mile Dike, built years ago when a cut-through was made to straighten the river's course. The southern arm of the lake is still a channel into the Mississippi, through which pass towboats pushing strings of barges loaded with gravel, sand, cotton, scrap iron, soybeans, fertilizer, or oil.

In August, the lake drops steadily lower, and at the foot of the levee mud flats begin to appear around the rusty barges that serve as Philippi's municipal terminal and around the old stern-wheeler moored just above them that has been converted into the Philippi Yacht Club. The surface of the mud, covered with discarded beer cans, broken bottles, and tangles of baling wire, cracks and scales like the skin of some scrofulous river beast, and a deathlike stench pervades the hot, still air. But the lake is deep and broad—more than a mile wide at the bend, close to the town—and fifty feet out from the lowest mud flat the steely surface water hides unplumbed black depths.

Later in August, if rain falls all along the course of the Mississippi, there will be a rise of the lake as the river backs into it. The mud flats are covered again. The trees put on pale spikes of new growth. The sandbars are washed clean. Mud runnels stream from the rain-heavy willow fronds, and the willows lift their heads. The fish begin to bite. For a week or two, from the crest of the rise, when the still water begins to clear, dropping the mud that the river has poured into the lake, until another drop has begun to expose the mud flats, Lake Okatukla is beautiful—a serene, broad wilderness of green trees and bright water, bounded at the horizon by the green range of levee sweeping in a slow curve against the sky.

Looking down into the water one can see through drifting forests of moss the quick flash of frightened bream, the shadowy threat of great saw-toothed gar. In the town, there has been little to do for weeks but wait out the heat. Only a few Negroes have braved the stench of the mud flats for the sake of a slimy catfish or a half-dead bream. After the rise, however, fishermen are out again in their skiffs, casting for bass around the trunks of the big willow trees or fishing with cane poles and minnows for white perch along the fringe willows. Family parties picnic here and there along the shore.

The lake is big—twelve miles long, with dozens of curving

inlets and white sandy islands. Hundreds of fishermen can spend their days trolling its shores and scarcely disturb one another.

* * *

One morning just after the August rise a few years ago, Anna Glover set out with two of her three sons, Ralph and Steve, and one of Ralph's friends, Murray McCrae, for a day on the lake. Her oldest son, who at fifteen considered himself too old for such family expeditions, and her husband, Richard, an architect, for whom summer was the busiest season of the year, had stayed behind.

It was early, and the waterfront was deserted when Anna drove over the crest of the levee. She parked the car close to the Yacht Club mooring float, where the Glovers kept their fishing skiff tied up, and began to unload the gear — life jackets for the children, tackle box, bait, poles, gas can, and Skotch cooler full of beer, soft drinks, and sandwiches. She had hardly begun when she thought she heard someone shouting her name.

"Miss Anna! Hey, Miss Anna!"

She looked around, but, seeing the whole slope of the levee empty and no one on the deck of the Yacht Club except Gaines Williamson, the Negro bartender, she called the children back from the water's edge, and began to distribute the gear among them to carry down to the float.

Anna heaved the heavy cooler out of the car without much effort and untied the poles from the rack on the side of the car, talking as she worked. At thirty-six, she looked scarcely old enough to have three half-grown sons. Her high, round brow was unlined, her brown eyes were clear, and her strong, boyish figure in shorts and a tailored shirt looked almost like a child's. She wore her long sandy-brown hair drawn into a twist on the back of her head.

Ralph and his friend Murray were ten; Steve was seven.

182

Ralph's straight nose, solemn expression, and erect, sway-backed carriage made him look like a small preacher. Steve was gentler, with brown eyes like his mother's, fringed by a breathtaking sweep of dark lashes. They were beautiful children, or so Anna thought, for she regarded them with the most intense, subjective passion.

Murray was a slender, dark boy with a closed face and a reserve that to Anna seemed impregnable. They were picking up the gear to move it down to the Yacht Club float when they all heard someone calling, and turned around.

"Ralph! Hey there, boys! Here I am, up here!" the voice cried.

"It's Estella, Mama," Ralph said. "There she is, over by the barges."

"Hi Estella!" Steve shouted. He and Ralph put down the poles and cooler and ran along the rough, uneven slope of the levee, jumping over the iron rings set in the concrete to hold the mooring lines and over the rusty cables that held the terminal barges against the levee.

"Come on, Murray," Anna said. "Let's go speak to Estella. She's over there fishing off the ramp."

Sitting on the galvanized-iron walkway from the levee to the terminal, her legs dangling over the side of the walkway ten feet above the oily surface of the water, was Estella Moseby, a huge and beautiful Negro woman who had worked for the Glover family since the children were small. She had left them a few months before to have a child and had stayed home afterward, at James', her husband's, insistence, to raise her own family. It was the first time that Anna or the children had seen her since shortly after the child was born.

Estella held a long cane pole in one hand and with the other waved toward Anna and the children. Her serene, round face was golden brown, the skin flawless even in the cruel light of the August sun, her black hair pulled severely back to a knot on her neck, her enormous dark eyes and wide mouth smiling with pleasure at the unexpected meeting. As the children approached, she drew her line out of the water and pulled herself up by the cable that served as a side rail for the walkway. The walk creaked under her shifting weight. She was fully five feet ten inches tall — at least seven inches taller than Anna — and loomed above the heads of the little group on the levee like an amiable golden giantess, her feet set wide apart to support the weight that fleshed her big frame. Her gaily flowered house dress, printed with daisies and morning-glories in shades of blue, green, and yellow, took on the very quality of her appearance, as if she were some tropical goddess robed to receive her worshippers.

"Lord, Estella," Anna said. "Come on down. We haven't seen you in ages. How have you been?"

"You see me," Estella said. "Fat as ever." She carefully wrapped her line around her pole, secured the hook in the cork, and came down from her high perch to join the others on the levee. "Baby or no baby, I got to go fishing after such a fine rain," she said.

"We're going on a picnic," Steve said.

"Well, isn't that fine," Estella said. "Where is your brother?"

"Oh, he thinks he's too old to associate with us any more," Anna said. "He *scorns* us. How is the baby?"

The two women looked at each other with the shy pleasure of old friends long separated who have not yet fallen back into the easy ways of their friendship.

"Baby's fine," Estella said. "My cousin Bernice is nursing him. I said to myself this morning, 'I haven't been fishing since I got pregnant with Lee Roy. I *got* to go fishing.' So look at me. Here I am sitting on this ramp since seven this morning and no luck."

"Yes, come on," Anna said. "Come on and keep me

company. You can't catch any fish around this old barge, and if you do they taste like fuel oil. I heard the bream are really biting in the upper lake — over on the other side, you know, in the willows."

Steve threw his arms around her legs. "Estella, why don't you come *work* for us again?" he said. "We don't like *anybody* but you."

"I'm coming, honey," she said. "Let me get these kids up a little bit and I'll be back."

"Estella, why don't you go fishing with us today?" Ralph said. "We're going up to the north end of the lake and fish all day."

"Yes, come on," Anna said. "Come on and keep me company. You can't catch any fish around this old barge, and if you do they taste like fuel oil. I heard the bream are really biting in the upper lake — over on the other side, you know, in the willows."

Estella hesitated, looking out over the calm and shining dark water. "I ain't much on boats," she said. "Boats make me nervous."

"Oh, come on, Estella," Anna said. "You know you want to go."

"Well, it's the truth, I'm not catching any fish sitting here. I got two little no-'count bream on my stringer." Estella paused, and then she said, "*All* y'all going to fish from the boat? I'll crowd you."

"We're going to find a good spot and fish off the bank," Anna said. "We're already too many to fish from the boat."

"Well, it'll be a pleasure," Estella said. "I'll just come along. Let me get my stuff." She went up on the walkway again and gathered up her tackle where it lay — a brown paper sack holding sinkers, floats, hooks, and line, and her pole and a coffee can full of worms and dirt.

"I brought my gig along," Ralph said as they all trudged

across the levee toward the Yacht Club. "I'm going to gig one of those great big buffalo or a gar or something."

"Well, if you do give it to me, honey," Estella said. "James is really crazy about buffalo the way I cook it." Pulling a coin purse out of her pocket, she turned to Anna. "You reckon you might get us some beer in the Yacht Club? A nice can of beer 'long about eleven o'clock would be good."

"I've got two cans in the cooler," Anna said, "but maybe we'd better get a couple more."

She took the money and, while Murray and Ralph brought the skiff around from the far side of the Yacht Club, where it was tied up, went into the bar and bought two more cans of beer. Estella and Steve, meanwhile, carried the fishing gear down to the float. Gaines Williamson, a short, powerfully built man in his forties, followed Anna out of the bar and helped stow their gear in the little boat. The children got in first and then he helped Estella in. "Lord, Miss Estella," he said, "you too big for this boat, and that's a fact." He stood back and looked down at her doubtfully, sweat shining on his face and standing in droplets on his shaven scalp.

"I must say it's none of your business," Estella said.

"We'll be all right, Gaines," Anna said. "The lake's smooth as glass."

* * *

The boys held the skill against the float while Anna got in, and they set out, cruising slowly up the lake until they found a spot that Estella and Anna agreed looked promising. Here, on a long, clean sandbar fringed with willows, they beached the boat. The children stripped off their life jackets, pulled off the jeans they wore over their swimming trunks, and began to wade.

"You children wade here in the open water," Estella

ordered. "Don't go over yonder on the other side of the bar, where the willows are growing. You'll bother the fish."

She and Anna stood looking around. Wilderness was all about them. As far as they could see on either side of the lake, not even a road ran down to the water's edge. While they watched, two white herons dragged themselves awkwardly into the air and flapped away, long legs trailing. The southern side of the sandbar, where they had beached the boat, had no trees growing on it, but the edge of the northern side, which curved in on itself and out again, was covered with willows. Here the land was higher. Beyond a low hummock crowned with cottonwood trees, Anna and Estella discovered a pool, twenty-five yards long and nearly as wide, that had been left behind by the last rise, a few days before. Fringe willows grew all around it, and the fallen trunk of a huge cottonwood lay with its roots exposed on the ground, its whole length stretched out into the still water of the pool.

"Here's the place," Estella said. "You sit down and rest yourself, Miss Anna."

"I'll come help you."

The two women unloaded the boat and Anna carried the cooler up the low hill and left it in the shade of one of the cottonwood trees. Then they gathered the fishing tackle and took it over to a shady spot by the pool. In a few minutes, the children joined them, and Anna passed out poles and bait. The bream were rising to crickets, and she had brought a wire cylinder basket full of them.

"You boys scatter out, now," Anna said. "There's plenty of room for everybody, and if you stay too close together you'll hook each other."

Estella helped Steve bait his hook, then baited her own and dropped it into the water as close as she could get it to the trunk of the fallen tree. Almost as soon as it reached the water, her float began to bob and quiver.

"Here we go," she said in a low voice. "Take it under, now. Take it under."

She addressed herself to the business of fishing with such delight and concentration that Anna stopped in the middle of rigging a pole to watch her. Even the children, intent on finding places for themselves, turned back to see Estella catch a fish. She stood over the pool like a priestess at her altar, all expectation and willingness, holding the pole lightly, as if her fingers could read the intentions of the fish vibrating through line and pole. Her bare arms were tense, and she gazed down into the still water.

A puff of wind made the leafy shadows waver and tremble on the pool, and the float rocked deceptively. Estella's arms quivered with a jerk begun and suppressed Her flowery dress flapped around her legs, and her skin shone with sweat and oil where the sunlight struck through the leaves across her forehead and down one cheek.

"Not yet," she muttered. "*Take* it." The float bobbed and went under. "Aah!"

She gave her line a quick, short jerk to set the hook; the line tightened, the long pole bent, and she swung a big bream out onto the sand. The fish flopped off the hook and down the slope toward the water; she dropped the pole and dived at it, half falling. Ralph who had been watching, was ahead of her, shouting with excitement, grabbing up the fish before it could flop back into the pool, and putting it into Estella's hands, careful to avoid the sharp dorsal fin.

"Look, boys, look!" she cried happily. "Just look at him!"

She held out the big bream, as wide and thick as her hand, marked with blue around the gills and orange on its swollen belly. The fish twisted and gasped in her hand while she got the stringer. She slid the metal end of the stringer through one gill and out the mouth, secured the other end to an exposed root of the fallen tree, and dropped the fish into the water, far enough away so that the bream's thrashing would not disturb their fishing spot.

"Quick now, Miss Anna," she said. "Get your line in there. I bet this pool is full of bream. Come on, boys, we're going to catch some fish today."

Anna baited her hook and dropped it in. The children scattered around the pool to their own places. In an hour, the two women had caught a dozen bream and four small catfish, and the boys had caught six or seven more bream.

Then for ten minutes no one got a bite, and the boys began to lose interest. A school of minnows flashed into the shallow water at Anna's feet, and she pointed them out to Estella. "Bream are gone," she said. "They've quit feeding, or we wouldn't see any minnows."

* * *

Anna laid down her pole and told the children they could swim. "Come on, Estella," she said. "We can sit in the shade and watch them and have a beer, and then in a little while we can move to another spot."

"You aren't going to let them swim in this old lake, are you, Miss Anna?" Estella said.

"Sure. The bottom's nice and sandy here," Anna said. "Murray, your mama said you've got to keep your life preserver on if you swim." She said to Estella in a low voice, "He's not much of a swimmer. He's the only one I would worry about."

The children splashed and tumbled fearlessly in the water, Ralph and Steve popping up and disappearing, sometimes for so long that Anna, in spite of what she had said, would begin to watch anxiously for their blond heads.

"I must say, I don't see how you stand it," Estella said. "That water scares me."

"Nothing to be scared of," Anna said. "They're both good swimmers, and so am I. I could swim across the lake and back, I bet you, old as I am."

She fished two beers out of the Skotch cooler, opened them, and gave one to Estella. Then she sat down with her back against a cottonwood tree, gave Estella a cigarette, took one herself, and leaned back with a sigh. Estella sat down on a fallen log, and the two women smoked and drank their beer in silence for a few minutes. The breeze ran through the cottonwoods, shaking the leaves against each other.

"I love the sound of the wind in a cottonwood tree," Anna said. "Especially at night when you wake up and hear it outside your window. I remember there was one outside the window of my room when I was a little girl, so close to the house I could climb out the window and get into it." The breeze freshened and the leaves pattered against each other. "It sounds cool," Anna said, "even in August."

"It's nice," Estella said. "Like a nice, light rain."

"Well, tell me what you've been doing with yourself," Anna said. "When are you going to move into your new house?"

"James wants to keep renting it out another year," Estella said. "He wants us to get ahead a little bit. And you know, Miss Anna, if I can hang on where I am we'll be in good shape. We can rent that house until we finish paying for it, and then when we move we can rent the one we're in, and, you know, we own that little one next door, too. With four children now, we got to think of the future. And I must say, with all his old man's ways, James is a good provider. He looks after his own. So I go along with him. But, Lord, I can't stand it much longer. We're falling all over each other in that little tiny place. Kids under my feet all day. No place to keep the baby quiet. And in rainy weather! It's worse than a circus. I've gotten so all I do is yell at the kids. It would be a rest to go back to work."

190

"I wish you *would* come back to work," Anna said.

"No use talking about it," Estella said. "James says I've got to stay home at least until Lee Roy gets up to school age. And you can see for yourself I'd be paying out half what I made to get somebody to keep mine. But I'll tell you, my nerves are tore up."

"It takes a while to get your strength back after a baby," Anna said.

"Oh, I'm strong enough," Estella said. "It's not that." She pulled a stalk of Johnson grass and began to chew it thoughtfully. "I've had something on my mind," she said, "something I've been meaning to tell you ever since the baby came, and I haven't see you by yourself—"

Anna interrupted her. "Look at the fish, Estella," she said. "They're really kicking up a fuss."

There was a wild, thrashing commotion in the water by the roots of the cottonwood tree where Estella had tied the stringer.

Estella watched a minute. "Lord, Miss Anna," she said, "Something's after those fish. A turtle or something." She got up and started toward the pool as a long, dark, whip-like shape flung itself out of the water, slapped the surface, and disappeared.

"Hey," Anna said, "it's a snake! A snake!"

Estella looked around for a weapon and hastily picked up a short, heavy stick and a rock from the ground. Moving lightly and easily in spite of her weight, she ran down to the edge of the water, calling over her shoulder, "I'll scare him off. I'll chunk him. Don't you worry."

She threw the rock into the churning water, but it had no effect. "Go snake. Leave our fish alone." She stood waving her stick threateningly over the water.

Anna came down to the pool now, and they both saw the whip-like form again. Fearlessly, Estella whacked at it with her stick.

"Keep back, Estella," Anna said. "He might bite you. Wait a minute and I'll get a longer stick."

"Go snake!" Estella shouted furiously, confidently. "What's the matter with him? He won't go off. Go, you crazy snake!"

Now the children heard the excitement and came running across the beach and over the low hill where Estella and Anna had been sitting, to see what was happening.

"A snake, a snake!" Steve screamed. "He's after the fish. Come on, y'all! It's a big old snake after the fish."

The two older boys ran up.

"Get'em out of the water, Mama," Ralph said. "He's going to eat 'em."

"I'm scared he might bite me," Anna said. "Keep back. He'll go away in a minute." She struck at the water with the stick she had picked up.

Murray looked the situation over calmly. "Why don't we gig him? He said to Ralph.

Ralph ran down to the boat and brought back the long, barb-pointed gig. "Move, Estella," he said. "I'm gonna gig him." He struck twice at the snake and missed.

"Estella," Ana said, "I saw his head. He can't go away. He's swallowed one of the fish. He's caught on the stringer." She shuddered with disgust. "What are we going to do?" she said. "Let's throw away the stringer. We'll never get him off."

"All them beautiful fish! No, *Ma'am*," Estella said. "Here, Ralph, he can't bite us if he's swallowed a fish. I'll untie the stringer and get up on land, and then you gig him."

"I'm going away," Steve said. "I don't what to watch." He crossed the hill and went back to the beach, where he sat down alone and began to dig a hole in the sand.

Ralph, wild with excitement, danced impatiently around Estella while she untied the stringer.

"Be calm, child," she said. She pulled the stringer out of the water and dropped it on the ground "Now!"

The snake had indeed tried to swallow one of the bream on the stringer. Its' jaws were stretched so wide as to look dislocated; its body was distended behind the head with the half-swallowed meal, and the fish's head could still be seen protruding from its mouth. The snake, faintly banded with slaty black on a brown background, was a water moccasin.

"Lord, it's a cottonmouth!" Estella cried as soon as she had the stringer out on land, where she could see the snake.

A thrill of horror and disgust raised the hair on Anna's arms. The thought of the helpless fish on the stringer sensing its enemy's approach, and then of the snake, equally and even more grotesquely helpless, filled her with revulsion. "Throw it away," she commanded. And then the thought of the stringer with its living burden of fish and snake struggling and swimming away into the lake struck her as even worse. "No!" she said. "Go on. Kill the snake, Ralph."

Ralph paid no attention to his mother but stood with the long gig poised, looking up at Estella for instructions

"Kill him," Estella said. "Now."

He drove the gig into the snake's body behind the head and pinned it to the ground, where it coiled and uncoiled convulsively, wrapping its tail around the gig and then unwrapping it and whipping it across the sand.

Anna mastered her horror as well as she could with a shake of her head. "Now what?" she said calmly.

Estella got a knife from the tackle box, held the dead but still writhing snake down with one big foot behind the gig on its body and the other on its tail, squatted, and deftly cut off the fish's head where it protruded from the gaping, fanged mouth. Then she worked the barbed point of the gig out of the body, picked the snake up on the point, and stood holding it away from her.

Ralph whirled around with excitement and circled Estella

twice. "We've killed a snake," he chanted. "We've killed a snake." We've killed a snake."

"Look at it wiggle," Murray said. "It keeps on wiggling even after it's dead."

"Yeah, a snake'll wiggle like that for an hour sometimes, even with its head cut off," Estella said. "Look out, Ralph."

She swept the gig forward through the air and threw the snake out into the pool, where it continued its aimless writhing on the surface of the water. She handed Ralph the gig and stood watching the snake for a few minutes, holding her hands away from her sides to keep the blood off her clothes. Then she bent down by the water's edge and washed the blood from her hands. She picked up the stringer, dropped the fish into the water, and tied the stringer to the root of the cottonwood. "There!" she said. "I didn't have no idea of throwing away all them — *those* beautiful fish. James would've skinned me if he ever heard about it."

Steve got up from the sand now and came over to his mother. He looked at the wigging snake, and then he leaned against his mother without saying anything, put his arms around her, and laid his head against her side.

Anna stroked his hair with one hand and held him against her with the other. "It was a moccasin, honey," she said. "They're poison, you know. You have to kill them."

"I'm hungry," Ralph said. "Is it time to eat?"

Anna shook her head, gave Steve a pat, and released him. "Let me smoke a cigarette first and forget about that old snake. Then we'll eat."

* * *

Anna and Estella went back to the shade on the hill and settled themselves once more, each with a fresh can of beer and a cigarette. The children retuned to the beach.

"I can do without snakes, Anna said. "Indefinitely."

194

Estella was still breathing hard. "I don't mind killing no snake," she said happily.

"I never saw anything like that before," Anna said. "A snake getting caught on a stringer, I mean. Did you?" Once or twice," Estella said. "And I've had 'em get after my stringer plenty of times."

"I don't see how you could stand to cut the fish's head off," Anna said, and shivered.

"Well, somebody had to."

"Yes, I suppose I would have done it if you hadn't been here." She laughed. "*Maybe*. I was mighty tempted to throw the whole thing away."

"I'm just as glad I wasn't pregnant," Estella said. "I'm glad it didn't happen while I was carrying Lee Roy. I would have been *helpless*."

"You might have had a miscarriage," Anna said. She laughed again, still nervous, wanting to stop talking about the snake but not yet able to, feeling somehow that there was more to be said. "Please don't have any miscarriages on fishing trips with me," she went on. "I can do without that, too."

"Miscarriage!" Estella said. "That's not what I'm talking about. And that reminds me, what I was getting ready to tell you when we saw the snake. You know, I said I had something on my mind?"

"Uh-huh."

"You remember last summer when you weren't home that day, and that kid fell out of the tree in the yard, and all?"

"How could I forget it?" Anna said.

"You remember you spoke to me so heavy about it? Why didn't I stay out in the yard with him until his mama got there, instead of leaving him laying on the ground like that, nobody with him but Ralph, and I told you I couldn't go out there to him — couldn't look at that kid with his leg broke, and all — and you didn't understand why?"

"Yes, I remember," Anna said.

"Well, I wanted to tell you I was *blameless*," Estella said. "I didn't want you to know it at the time, but I was pregnant. I *couldn't* go out there. It might have *marked* my child, don't you see? I might have bore a cripple."

"Oh, Estella! You don't believe that kind of foolishness do you?" Anna said.

"*Believe* it? I've seen it happen," Estella said. "I know it's true." She was sitting on the fallen log, so that she towered above Anna, who had gone back to her place on the ground, leaning against the tree. Now Estella leaned forward with an expression of intense seriousness on her face. "My aunt looked on a two-headed calf when she was carrying a child," she said, "and her child had six fingers on one hand and seven on the other."

Anna hitched herself up higher, then got up and sat down on the log beside Estella. "But that was an accident," she said. "A coincidence. Looking at the calf didn't have anything to do with it."

Estella shook her head stubbornly. "This world is a mysterious place," she said. "Do you think you can understand everything in it?"

"No," Anna said. "Not everything. But I don't believe in magic."

"All this world is full of mystery," Estella repeated. "You got to be brave and times when you go down helpless in spite of all. Like that snake. You were afraid of that snake."

"I thought it might bite me," Anna said. "And besides, it was so horrible the way he was caught."

But Estella went on as if she hadn't heard. "You see," she said, "there are things you overlook. Things, I was telling you about my aunt, that are *true*. My mother in her day saw more wonders than that. She knew more than one that sickened and died of a spell. And this child with the fingers, I know about him for a fact. I lived with them when I was teaching school. I lived in the house with that kid. So I'm not taking any chances."

"But I thought you had lost your head and got scared because he was hurt," Anna said. "When the little boy broke his leg, I mean. I kept thinking it wasn't like you. That's what really happened, isn't it?"

"No," Estella said. "It was like I told you."

Anna said no more, but sat quiet a long time, lighting another cigarette and smoking calmly, her face expressionless. But her thoughts were in a tumult of exasperation, bafflement, and outrage. She tried unsuccessfully to deny, to block out, the overriding sense of the difference between herself and Estella, borne in on her by this strange conversation so foreign to their quiet, sensible friendship. She had often thought, with pride both in herself and in Estella, what an accomplishment their friendship was, knowing how much delicacy of feeling, how much consideration and understanding they had both brought to it. And now it seemed to her that it was this very friendship, so carefully nurtured for years, that Estella had unwittingly attacked.

With a few words, she had put between them all that separated them, all the dark and terrible past. In the tumult of Anna's feelings there rose a queer, long-forgotten memory of a nurse she had once had as a child — the memory of a brown hand thrust out at her, holding a greasy black ball of hair combings. "You see, child, I saves my hair. I ain't never th'owed away a hair of my head."

"Why?" she had asked.

"Bad luck to th'ow away combings. Bad luck to lose any part of yourself in this old world. Fingernail parings, too. I gathers them up and carries them home and burns them. And I sits by the fire and watches until every last little bitty hair is turned plumb to smoke."

"But why?" she had asked again.

"Let your enemy possess one hair of your head and you will be in his power," the nurse had said. She had thrust the hair ball into her apron pocket, and now, in the memory, she seemed to be brushing Anna's hair, and Anna remembered standing restive under her hand, hating, as always, to have her hair brushed.

"Hurry up," she had said. "All right, honey. I'm through." The nurse had given her head one last lick and then, bending toward her, still holder her arm while she struggled to be off and outdoors again, had thrust a dark, brooding face close to hers, had looked at her for a long, scary moment, and had laughed.

"I saves your combings, too, honey. You in my power."

With an effort Anna drew herself up short. She put out her cigarette, threw her beer can into the lake, and stood up.

"I reckon we better fix some lunch," she said. "The children are starving."

* * *

By the time they had finished lunch, burned the discarded papers, thrown the bread crusts and crumbs of potato chips to the birds, and put the empty soft-drink bottles back in the cooler, it had begun to look like rain. Anna stood gazing thoughtfully into the sky. "Maybe we ought to start back," she said, "We don't want to get caught in the rain up here."

"Were not going to catch any more fish as long as the wind is blowing," Estella said.

"We want to swim some more," Ralph said.

"You can't go swimming right after lunch," Anna said. "You might get a cramp. And it won't be any fun to get caught in the rain. We'd better call it a day." She picked up one of the poles and began to wind the line around it. "Come on kids," she said. "Let's load up."

They loaded their gear into the skiff and dropped the stringer full of fish in the bottom. Ana directed Murray and Steve to sit in the bow, facing the stern. Estella got in cautiously and took the middle seat. Anna and Ralph waded in together, pushed the skiff off the sandbar, and then got into the stern.

"You all got your life jackets on?" Anna said glancing at the boys. "That's right."

Ralph pulled on the recoil-starter rope until he had got the little motor started, and they headed down the lake. The heavily loaded skiff showed no more than eight inches of freeboard, and as they cut through the choppy water, waves sprayed over the bow and sprinkled Murray and Steve. Anna moved the tiller and headed the skiff in closer to the shore.

"We'll stay close in going down," she said. "Water's not so rough in here. And then we can cut across the lake right opposite the Yacht Club."

Estella sat still in the middle of the skiff, her back to Anna, hand on each gunwale, as they moved steadily down the lake, rocking with the wind-rocked waves. "I don't like this old lake when it's windy," Estella said. "I don't like no windy water."

When they reached a point opposite the Yacht Club, where the lake was a little more than a mile wide, Anna headed the skiff into the rougher open water. The wind, however, was still no more than a stiff breeze, and the skiff was a quarter of the way across the lake before Anna began to be worried.

Spray from the choppy waves was coming in more and more often over the bow; Murray and Steve were drenched, and an inch of water sloshed in the bottom of the skiff. Estella had not spoken since she had said "I don't like no windy water." She sat perfectly still, gripping the gunwales with both hands, her paper sack of tackle in her lap, her worm can on the seat beside her.

Suddenly a gust of wind picked up the paper sack and blew it out of the boat. It struck the water and floated back to Anna, who reached out, picked it up, and dropped it by her own feet.

Estella did not move, although the sack brushed against her face as it blew out. She made no attempt to catch it. She's scared, Anna thought. She's so scared she didn't even see it blow away. And Anna was frightened herself. She leaned forward, picked up the worm can from the seat beside Estella, dumped out the worms and dirt, and tapped Estella on the shoulder.

"Here," she said "Why don't you bail some of the water out of the bottom of the boat, so your feet won't get wet?"

Estella did not look around, but reached over her shoulder, took the can, and began to bail, still holding to the gunwale tightly with her left hand.

The wind freshened, the waves began to show white at their tips, the clouds in the south raced across the sky, darker and darker. But still, although they could see sheets of rain far away to the south, the sun shone on them brightly. They were now almost halfway across the lake. Anna looked over her shoulder toward the quieter water they had left behind. Along the shore of the lake, the willow trees tossed in the wind like a forest of green plumes.

It's just as far one way as the other, she thought, and anyhow there's nothing to be afraid of. But while she looked back, the board slipped off course, no longer quartering the waves, and immediately they took a big one over their bow.

"Bail, Estella," Anna said quietly, putting the boat back on course. "Get that water out of the boat. Her mind was filled with one paralyzing thought: She can't swim. My God, Estella can't swim.

"Estella," she said, "the boat will not sink. It may fill up with water, but it won't sink. Do you understand? It is all filled with cork, like a life preserver. It won't sink, do you hear me?"

She repeated herself louder and louder above the wind.

Estella sat with her back turned and bailed. She did not move or answer, or even nod her head. She went on bailing frantically, mechanically, dumping pint after pint of water over the side while they continued to ship waves over the bow. Murray and Steve sat in their places and stared at Anna. Ralph sat motionless by her side. No one said a word.

I've got to take care of them all, Anna thought. Estella kept wallowing now, hardly moving before the labored push of the motor. Estella gave a yell and started to rise, holding to the gunwales with both hands.

"Sit down, you fool!" Anna shouted. "Sit *down!*"

"We're gonna sink!" Estella yelled. "And I can't swim, Miss Anna! I can't swim!" For the first time, she turned, and stared at Anna with wild, blind eyes. She stood all the way up and clutched the air. "I'm gonna drown!" she yelled.

The boat rocked and settled, the motor drowned out, another wave washed in over the bow, and the boat tipped slowly up on it side. An instant later, they were all in the water and the boat was floating upside down beside them.

The children bobbed up immediately, buoyant in their life jackets. Anna glanced around once to see if they were all there. "Stay close to the boat, boys," she said.

And then Estella heaved out of the water, fighting frantically, eyes vacant, mouth open, the broad expanse of her golden face set in mindless desperation.

Anna got hold of one of the handgrips at the stem of the boat and, with her free hand, grabbed Estella's arm. "You're all right," she said. "Come on, I've got hold of the boat."

She tried to pull the huge bulk of the Negro woman toward her and guide her hand to the grip. Estella did not speak, but lunged forward in the water with a strangled yell and three herself on Anna, flinging her arms across her shoulders. Anna felt herself sinking and scissors-kicked strongly to keep herself up, but she went down.

Chin-deep in the water, she threw back her head and took a breath before Estella pushed her under. She hung on to the grip with all her strength, feeling herself battered against the boat and jerked away from it by Estella's struggle. This can't be happening, she thought. We can't be out here drowning. She felt a frantic hand brush across her face and snatch at her nose and hair. My glasses, she thought as she felt them torn away, and she, too, went under. Then both women came up and Anna got hold of Estella's arm again.

"Come *on*," she gasped. "The *boat*."

Again Estella threw herself forward, the water streaming from her head and shoulders. This time Anna pulled her close enough to get hold of the grip, but Estella did not try to grasp it. Her hand slid, clawing, along Anna's wrist and arm; again she somehow rose up in the water and came down on Anna, and again the two women went under.

This time, Estella's whole thrashing bulk was above Anna; she held with all her strength to the handgrip, but felt herself torn away from it. She came up behind Estella, who was now clawing frantically at the side of the skiff, which sank down on their side and tipped gently toward them as she pulled at it.

Anna ducked down and somehow got her shoulder against Estella's rump. Kicking and heaving with a strength she did not possess. She boosted Estella up and forward so that she fell sprawling across the boat.

"*There!*" She came up as the rocking skiff began to submerge under Estella's weight.

"Stay there!" she gasped. "*Stay* on it. For God's . . ."

But the boat was under a foot of water now, rocking and slipping away under Estella's shifting weight. Clutching and kicking crazily, mouth open in a soundless prolonged scream, eyes staring, she slipped off the other side, turned her face toward Anna, gave a strange, strangled grunt, and sank again. The water churned and foamed where she had been.

Anna swam around the boat toward her. As she swam, she realized that Ralph and Steve were screaming for help. Murray floated in the water with a queer, embarrassed smile on his face, as if he had been caught at something shameful. "I'm not here," he seemed to be saying. "This is all just an embarrassing mistake."

By the time Anna got to Estella, the boat was a couple of yards away—too far, she knew, for her to try to get Estella back to it. Estella broke the surface of the water directly in front of her and immediately flung both arms around her neck. Nothing Anna had ever learned in a lifesaving class seemed to have any bearing on the reasonless two hundred pounds of flesh with which she had to deal. They went down.

This time they stayed under so long, deep in the softly yielding black water, that Anna thought she would not make it back up. Her very brain seemed ready to burst out of her ears and nostrils. She scissors-kicked again and again with all her strength — not trying to pull loo0se from Estella's clinging but now more passive weight — and they came up. Anna's head was thrust up and back, ready for a breath, and the instant she felt the air on her face, she took it, deep and gulping, swallowing some water at the same time, and they went down again.

Estella's arms rested heavily — trustingly, it seemed — on her shoulders. She did not hug Anna or try to strangle her but simply kept holding on and pushing her down. This time, again deep in the dark water, when Anna raised her arms for a strong down stroke, she touched a foot.

One of the boys was floating above their heads. She grabbed the foot without a thought and pulled with all her strength, scissors-kicking at the same time. She and Estella popped out of the water. Gasping in the life-giving air, Anna found herself staring into Steve's face as he floated beside her, weeping.

My God, I'll drown him if he doesn't get out of the way, she thought. I'll drown my own child. But she had no time to say even a word to warn him before they went down again.

The next time up, she heard Ralph's voice, high and shrill and almost in her ear, and realized that he, too, was swimming close by, and was pounding on Estella's shoulder.

"Estella, let go, let go!" he was crying. "Estella, you're drowning Mama!"

Estella did not hear. She seemed not even to try to raise her head or breathe when their heads broke out of the water.

Once more they went under and came up before Anna thought, I've given out. There's no way to keep her up, and nobody is coming. And then, deep in the lake, the brassy taste of fear on her tongue, the yielding water pounding in her ears: She's going to drown me. I've got to let her drown, or she will drown me. She drew her knee up under her chin, planted her foot in the soft belly, still swollen from pregnancy, and shoved as hard as she could, pushing herself up and back and Estella down and away. Estella was not holding her tightly, and it was easy to push her away. The big arms slid off Anna's shoulders, the limp hands making no attempt to clutch or hold.

They had been together, close as lovers in the darkness or as twins in the womb of the lake, and now they were apart. Anna shot up into the air with the force of her shove and took a deep, gasping breath. Treading water, she waited for Estella to come up beside her, but nothing happened. The three children floated in a circle and looked at her. A vision passed through her mind of Estella's body drifting downward, downward through layers of increasing darkness, all her golden strength and flowery beauty mud-and-water-dimmed, still aimless as a drifting log. I ought to surface-dive and look for her, she thought, and the thought of going down again turned her bowels to water.

Before she had to decide to dive, something nudged lightly against her hand, like an inquiring, curious fish. She grabbed at it and felt the inert mass of Estella's body, drained of struggle, floating below the surface of the water. She got hold of the belt of her dress and pulled.

Estella's back broke the surface of the water, mounded and rocking in the dead man's float, and then sank gently down again. Anna held on to the belt. She moved her feet tiredly to keep herself afloat and looked around her. I can't even get her face out of the water, she thought. I haven't the strength to lift her head.

* * *

The boat was floating ten yards away. The Skotch cooler, bright red-and-black plaid, bobbed gaily in the water nearby. Far, far off she could see the levee. In the boat it had looked so near and the distance across the lake so little that she had said she could easily swim it, but now everything in the world except the boat, the children, and this lifeless body was unthinkably far away. Tiny black figures moved back and forth along the levee, people going about their business without a thought of tragedy. The whole sweep of the lake was empty, with not another boat in sight except the Gay Rosey Jane, still moving up the channel.

All that had happened had happened so quickly that the towboat seemed no nearer than it had before the skiff overturned. Murray floated in the water a few yards off, still smiling his embarrassed smile. Steve and Ralph stared at their mother with stricken faces. The sun broke through the shifting blackness of the sky, and at the same time a light rain began to fall, pattering on the choppy surface of the lake and splashing into their faces.

All her senses dulled and muffled by shock and exhaustion, Anna moved her feet and worked her way toward the boat, dragging her burden.

"She's gone," Steve said. "Estella's drowned." Tears and rain streamed down his face.

"What shall we do, Mama?" Ralph said.

Dimly, Anna realized that he had sensed her exhaustion and was trying to rouse her.

"Yell," she said. "All three of you yell. Maybe somebody . . ." The children screamed for help again and again, their thin, piping voices floating away in the wind.

With her last strength, Anna continued to work her way toward the boat, pulling Estella after her. She swam on her back, frog-kicking, and feeling the inert bulk bump against her legs at every stroke. When she reached the boat, she took hold of the handgrip and concentrated on holding on to it.

"What shall we do?" Ralph said again. "They can't hear us."

Overcome with despair, Anna let her head droop toward the water. "No one is coming," she said. "It's too far. They can't hear you." And then, from somewhere, dim thoughts of artificial respiration, of snatching back the dead, came into her mind and she raised her head. Still time. I've got to get her out now, she thought.

"Yell again," she said.

"I'm going to swim to shore and get help," Ralph said. He looked toward his mother for a decision, but his face clearly showed that he knew he could not expect one. He started swimming away, his blond head bobbling in the rough water. He did not look back.

"I don't know," Anna said. Then she remembered vaguely that in an accident you were supposed to stay with the boat. "She's dead," she said to herself. "My God, she's dead. My fault."

Ralph swam on, the beloved head smaller and smaller on the vast expanse of the lake. The Gay Rosey Jane moved steadily up the channel. They might run him down, Anna thought. They'd never see him. She opened her mouth to call him back.

"Somebody's coming!" Murray shouted. "They see us. Somebody's coming. Ralph!"

Ralph heard him and turned back, and now they saw two boats racing toward them, one from the Yacht Club and one from the far side of the lake, across the terminal. In the nearer one they saw Gaines Williamson.

Thirty yards away, something happened to Gaines' engine; it raced, ground, and died. Standing in the stern of the rocking boat, he worked frantically over it while they floated and watched. It could not have been more than a minute or two before the other boat pulled up beside them, but every moment that passed, Anna knew, might be the moment of Estella's death.

In the stern of the second boat they saw a wiry white man wearing a T-shirt and jeans. He cut his engine when he was beside them, and, moving quickly to the side of the boat near Anna, bent over her in great excitement.

"Are you all right?" he asked. He grabbed her arms with a hard, calloused hand and shook her as if he had seen that she was about to pass out. "Are you all right?" he asked again, his face close to hers.

Anna stared at him, scarcely understanding what the question meant. The children swam over to the boat, and he helped them in and then turned back to Anna. "Come on," he said, and took hold of her arm again. "You've got to help yourself. Can you make it?"

"Get this one first," she said.

"What?" He stared at her with a queer, concentrated gaze, and she realized that he had not even seen Estella.

She hauled on the belt, and Estella's back broke the surface of the water, rolling, rocking, and bumping against the side of the boat. "I've got somebody else here," she said.

He grunted as if someone had hit him in the stomach. Reaching down, he grabbed the back of Estella's dress, pulled her toward her, got one hand into her hair, raised her face out of the water, and, bracing himself against the gunwale, held her there. Estella's peaceful face turned slowly toward him. Her mouth and eyes were closed, her expression was one of deep repose. The man stared at her and then at Anna.

"My God," he said.

"We've got to get her into the boat," Anna said. "If we can get her where we can give her artificial respiration . . ."

"It's Estella," Steve said. "Mama had her all the time." He began to cry again. "Let go of her hair," he said. "You're hurting her."

The three children shifted all at once to the side of the boat where the man was still holding Estella, and he turned on them sternly. "Get back," he said. "Sit *down*. And sit still."

The children scuttled back to their places. "You're hurting her," Steve said again.

"It's all right, son." The man said. "She can't feel a thing." To Anna, in a lower voice, he said, "She's dead."

"I'll push and you pull," Anna said. "Maybe we can get her into the boat."

He shifted his position, bracing himself as well as he could into the rocking boat, rested Estella's head on his own shoulder, and put both arms around her. They heaved and pushed at the limp body, but they could not get her into the boat. The man let her down into the water again, this time holding her under the arms. A hundred yards away, Gaines still struggled with his engine.

"Hurry up!" the man shouted. "Get on over here. We can't lift this woman by ourselves."

"Fishing lines tangled in the screw!" Gaines shouted back. His engine caught and died again.

"We're going to have to tow her in," the man said. "That fellow can't start his boat." He reached behind him and got a life jacket. "We'd better put this on her," he said. They worked Estella's arms into the life jacket and fastened the straps. "I've got a rope here somewhere," he said. "Hold her a minute. Wait." He handed Anna a life jacket. "You put this one on, too."

While he still held Estella by the hair, Anna struggled into the life jacket, and then took hold of the straps of Estella's. Just then, Gaines got his engine started, raced across the open water, and drew up beside them.

The two boats rocked in the rough water with Anna and Estella between them. Anna, with a hand on the gunwale of each, held them apart while the two men, straining and grunting, hauled Estella's body up out of the water and over the gunwale of Gaines' boat. Gaines heaved her legs in. She flopped, face down, across the seat and lay with one arm hanging over the side, the hand trailing in the water.

Anna lifted the arm and put it in the boat. Then the white man pulled Anna into his boat. As he helped her over the side, she heard a smacking blow, and, looking back, saw that Gaines had raised and turned Estella's body and was pounding her in the belly. Water poured out of her mouth and, in reflex, air rushed in.

The boats roared off across the lake toward the Yacht Club. The white man's was much the faster of the two, and he quickly pulled away. As soon as they were within calling distance, he stood up in the boat and began to yell at the little group gathered on the Yacht Club mooring float.

"Drowned! She's drowned!" he yelled. "Call an ambulance Get a resuscitator down here. Hurry!"

* * *

They drew up to the float. He threw a rope to one of the Negroes standing there and jumped out. Anna dragged herself to a sitting position and stared stupidly at the crowd of Negroes. Gaines Williamson pulled up behind them in the other boat.

"Give us a hand," the white man said. "Let's get her out of there. My God, she's huge. Somebody lend a hand."

To Anna it seemed that all the rest of the scene on the float took place above and far away from her. She saw legs moving back and forth, heard voices and snatches of conversation, felt herself moved from one place to another, but nothing that happened interrupted her absorption in grief and guilt. For the time, nothing existed for her except the belief that Estella was dead.

Someone took her arm and helped her onto the float while the children climbed up by themselves. She sat down on the splintery boards, surrounded by legs, and no one paid any attention to her.

"I saw 'em." The voice of a Negro woman in the crowd. "I

was setting on the levee and I saw 'em. You heard me. 'My Lord save us, some folks out there drowning.' I said. I was up on the levee and I run down to the Yacht Club . . ."

"Did somebody call an ambulance?" the white man asked.

"I run down here to the Yacht Club, like to killed myself running, and . . ."

"How . . ."

"Gay Rosey Jane swamped them. Never even seen them. Them towboats don't stop for nobody. See, there she goes. Never seen them at all."

"Still got a stitch in my side. My Lord, I liked to killed myself running . . ."

"Anybody around here know to give artificial respiration?"

"I was sitting right yonder on the terminal fishing with her this morning. Would you believe that?"

"God have mercy on us."

"Oh, Lord. Oh, Lord God. Lord God."

"Have mercy on us."

A young Negro in Army khakis walked over to where the white man and Gaines Williamson were trying to get Estella out of the bulky jacket.

"We'll cut it off," he said calmly. He pulled a straight razor from his pocket, slit one shoulder of the life jacket, pushed it out of the way, and straddled Estella's body.

"I know how," he said. "I learned in the Army."

He arranged her body in position — flying flat on her stomach, face turned to the side and arms above her head — and set to work, raising her arms and then her body rhythmically. When he lifted her body in the middle, her face dragged on the splintery planks of the float.

Anna crawled through the crowd to where Estella lay. Squatting down without a word, she put her hands under Estella's face to protect it from the splinters. It passed through her mind that she should do something about the children.

Looking around, she saw them standing in a row at one

side of the float, staring.

Somebody ought to get them away from here, she thought vaguely, but the thought left her mind and she forgot them. She swayed, rocked back on her heels, sat down suddenly, and then lay on her stomach, her head against Estella's head, her hands cradling the sleeping face.

Who's going to tell James, she thought. Who's going to tell him she's dead? And then I. I have to tell him. She began to talk to Estella. "Please darling," she said. "Please, Estella, breathe." Tears of weakness rolled down her face, and she looked up above the forest of legs at the black faces in a circle around them. "She's got four babies," she said. "Babies. Who's going to tell her husband she's dead? Who's going to tell him?" And then, again, "Please Estella, breathe. Please breathe."

No one answered. The young Negro soldier continued to raise the limp arms and body alternately, his motions deliberate and rhythmical, the sweat pouring off his face and dripping down on his sweat-soaked shirt. His thin face was intent and stern. The sun had come out and beat down bright and hot, raising steamy air from the rain-soaked float.

A long time passed. The soldier giving Estella artificial respiration looked around at the crowd. "Anybody know how to do this? I'm about to give out." He did not pause or break the rhythm of his motions.

A man stepped out of the crowd. "I can do it," he said. "I know how."

"Come on then," the soldier said. "Get down here by me and do it with me three times, and then, when I stop, you take over. Don't break it."

"Please, Estella," Anna said. "Please."

"One . . . Two . . ."

She felt someone pulling at her arm and looked up. A policeman was standing over her. "Here, lady," he said. "Get up off that dock. You ain't doing no good."

"But the splinters will get in her face," Anna said. "I'm

211

holding her face off the boards."

"It ain't going to matter if her face is tore up if she's dead," the policeman said. "Get up."

Someone handed her a towel, and she folded it and put it under Estella's face. The policeman dragged her to her feet and took her over to a chair near the edge of the float and sat her down in it. He squatted beside her. "Now, who was in the boat?" he said. "I got to make a report."

Anna made a vague gesture. "We were," she said.

"Who is 'we,' lady?"

"Estella and I and the children."

"Lady, give me the names, please," the policeman said.

"Estella Moseby, the Negro woman. She used to work for me, and we asked her, we asked her —" she broke off.

"Come on, who else?"

Anna stared at him, a short, bald man with shining pink scalp, and drum belly buttoned tightly into his uniform. A wave of nausea overcame her, and she saw his head surrounded by the shimmering black spokes of a rimless wheel, a black halo. "I'm going to be sick," she said. Collapsing out of the chair onto the dock, she leaned her head over the edge and vomited into the lake.

He waited until she was through and then helped her back into her chair. "Who else was with you?" he said.

"My two children, Ralph and Steve," she said. "Murray McCrae. I am Mrs. Richard Glover."

"Where is this McCrae fellow? He all right?"

"He's a little *boy*," Anna said. "A child. He's over there somewhere."

"You sure there wasn't nobody else with you?"

"No, that's all," Anna said.

"Now give me the addresses, please. Where did the nigger live?"

"For God's sake," Anna said. "What difference does it make? Go away and let me alone."

"I got to make my report, lady."

Ralph tugged at Anna's arm. "Mama, hadn't I better call Daddy?" he said.

"Yes," she said. "Yes, I guess you had." Oh God, she thought, he has to find out. I can't put it off. Everybody has to find out that Estella is dead."

Anna heard a commotion on the levee. The steadily increasing crowd separated, and two white-jacketed men appeared and began to work over Estella. Behind them, a woman with a camera snapped pictures.

"What are they taking *pictures* of her for?" Anna asked.

Then she heard her husband's voice shouting, "Get off the damn raft, God damn it! Get off. You want to sink it? Get back here. You want to drown us all."

The policeman stood up and went toward the crowd. "What the hell?" Anna heard him say.

"And put that camera up, if you don't want me to throw it in the lake." Anna's husband was in a fury of outrage, and concentrated it for the moment on the woman reporter from the local newspaper, who was snapping pictures of Estella.

"You all right, Anna?" Richard asked her.

The people on the float were scuttling back to the levee, and the reporter had disappeared. Anna, who was still sitting where the policeman had left her, nodded and opened her mouth to speak, but her husband was gone before she could say anything. She felt a wave of self-pity. He didn't even stay to help me, she thought.

Then, a moment or an hour later — she did not know how long — she heard a strange high-pitched shriek from the other end of the float. What's that, she thought. It sounded again — a long, rasping rattle and then a shriek. Does the machine they brought make that queer noise?

"She's breathing," somebody said.

"No," Anna said aloud to nobody, for nobody. "Who's going to tell James?"

The float was cleared now Besides Estella and Anna, only the two policemen, the two men from the ambulance, and Gaines Williamson were on it. The man who had rescued them was gone. The crowd stood quietly on the levee.

"Where is Richard?" Anna said. "Did he leave?"

No one answered.

The long, rasping rattle and shriek sounded again. Gaines Williamson came over to where Anna was sitting, and bent down to her, smiling kindly. "She's alive, Mrs. Glover," he said. "She's going to be all right."

Anna shook her head.

"Yes, Ma'am. She's moving and breathing, and yelling like crazy. She's going to be all right."

Anna got up shakily. She walked over to where the men were working Estella onto a stretcher.

"What's she doing?" she said. "What's the matter with her?"

Estella was thrashing her arms and legs furiously, mouth open, eyes staring, her face again the mask of mindless terror that Anna had seen in the lake The rattle and shriek were her breathing and screaming.

"She must think she's still in the water," one of the men said. "Shock. But she's O.K. Look at her kick."

Anna sat down on the float, her knees buckling under her, and someone pulled her out of the way while four men carried the stretcher off the float and up the levee toward the ambulance.

Richard reappeared at the foot of the levee and crossed the walkway to the Yacht Club. He bent down to help her up. "I'm sorry I had to leave you," he said. "I had to get the children away from here and find someone to take them home."

"My God," Anna said. "She's alive. They said she would be all right."

Later, in the car, she said to her husband, "She kept pushing me down, Richard. I tried to hold her up, I tried to make her take hold of the boat. But she kept pushing me down."

"It's all right now," he said. "Try not to think about it any more."

* * *

The next day, when Anna visited Estella in the hospital, she learned that Estella remembered almost nothing of what had happened. She recalled getting into the skiff for the trip home, but everything after that was gone.

"James says you saved my life," she said, in a hoarse whisper, "and I thank you."

Her husband stood at the head of her bed, gray-haired and signified in his Sunday suit. He nodded. "The day won't come when we'll forget it, Miss Anna," he said. "God be my witness."

Anna shook her head. "I never should have taken you out without a life preserver," she said.

"Ain't she suppose to be a grown woman?" James said. "She suppose to know better herself."

"How do you feel?" Anna asked.

"Lord, not a square inch on my body don't ache," Estella said. She laid her hands on the mound of her body under the sheet. "My stomach!" she said, with a wry laugh. "Somebody must've jumped up and down on it."

"I reckon that's from the artificial respiration," Anna said. "I had never seen anyone do it that way before. They pick you up under the stomach and then put you down and lift your arms. And then, too, I kicked you. And we must have banged you up some getting you into the boat. Lord! The more I think about it, the worse it gets. Because Gaines hit you in the stomach, too, as soon as he got you into the boat. That's what really saved your life. As soon as he got you into the boat, he hit you in the stomach and got rid of a lot of the water in your lungs and let in some air. I believe that breath you took in Gaines' boat kept you alive until we got you to the dock."

"You kicked me?" Estella said.

"We were going down," Anna said, feeling that she must confess to Estella the enormity of what she had done, "and I finally knew I couldn't keep you up. I kicked you in the stomach hard, and got loose from you, and then when you came up I grabbed you and held on, and about that time they saw us and the boats came. You passed out just when I kicked you, or else the kick knocked you out because you didn't struggle any more. I reckon that was lucky, too."

Estella shook her head. "I can't remember anything about it," she whispered. "Not anything." She pointed out the window toward the smokestack rising from the opposite wing of the hospital. "Seems like last night I got the idea there's a little man up there," she said. "He peeps out from behind that smokestack at me, and I'm afraid of him. He leans on the smokestack and then he jumps away real quick, like it's hot, and one time he came right over here and stood on the window ledge and looked in at me. Lucky the window was shut. I said 'Boo!' and, you know, he fell off! It didn't hurt him; he came right back. He wants to tell me something, yes, but he can't get in."

She closed her eyes.

Anna looked anxiously at James.

"They still giving her something to keep her quiet," he said. "Every so often she gets a notion somebody trying to get in here."

Estella opened her eyes. "I thank you, Miss Anna," she said. "James told me you saved my life." She smiled. "Seems like every once in a while I hear your voice," she said. "Way off. Way, way off. You're saying, 'I'll save you, Estella. Don't be afraid. I'll save you.' That's all I can remember."

* * *

Ellen Douglas / *The New Yorker,* © *Conde Nast.* Used with permission. Ellen Douglas (1921 – 2012) was born Josephine Ayres and grew up in Hope, Arkansas and Alexandria, Louisiana, but spent summers with her grandparents in Natchez, Mississippi, before getting a degree at the University of Mississippi and settling in Greenville, Mississippi with her husband Kenneth Haxton. She chose the penname of Ellen Douglas because she didn't want to embarrass her family by writing about family and racial issues. A 1973 National Book Award nominee, her books include *A Family's Affairs, Can't Quit You Baby,* and *The Rock Cried Out.* She was writer-in-residence at the University of Mississippi from 1979 to 1983. One of her creative writing students was Larry Brown, who is featured in *Mojo Rising* (Volume II).

ACKNOWLEDGEMENTS

In addition to the two individuals mentioned on the dedication page, I would like to thank the following for their help with this project: Robert Shatzkin, permissions coordinator at Liveright Publishing Corporation and W.W. Norton & Company; Yessenia Santos, senior permissions manager at Simon & Schuster; Sherri Hinchey, permissions manager at Penguin Random House; Annie Kronenberg, permission agent at John Hawkins & Associates; Abby Muller, permissions director at Algonquin Books of Chapel Hill; Rob McQuilkin and Eve Gleichman at Russell & Volkening; Christopher Wait, permissions director at New Directions Publishing; Ronald Hussey, director of permissions at Houghton Mifflin Harcourt; permissions department at HarperCollins; JoAnne Prichard Morris and David Rae Morris; Rosie Norwood-Kelly at the Cartoon Bank for The New Yorker; Scott Gould of RLR Associates; Huger Foote, for sending the photograph he took of his father in Paris; Cristina Concepcion at Don Congdon Associates; Ayres Haxton, for selecting a photograph of his mother, Ellen Douglas; Mary Alice White, director of the Eudora Welty House, for selecting a photograph of her aunt, Eudora Welty; Robert H. Brinkmeyer, Jr., Director, Institute for Southern Studies, University of South Carolina; Robert W. Hamblin, Professor Emeritus of English and Founding Director, Center for Faulkner Studies, Southeast Missouri State University; Peter Cooley, Professor of English, Director of Creative Writing, Tulane University; special thanks to William Griffith, Curator of Rowan Oak, University of Mississippi; Rambling Steve Gardner, who shot the cover image in the 1970s at Silver City, Mississippi (the house no longer exists) and University of Mississippi journalism professor Joseph B. Atkins, who served as editor of *Mojo Rising,* Volume II (working with a dozen writers on a single project is a little like herding cats, but without the purring reinforcement).

Mojo Rising: Masters of the Art

IF YOU ENJOYED THIS BOOK, WE ENCOURAGE YOU
TO READ THE SECOND VOLUME IN OUR ANTHOLOGY
SERIES: *MOJO RISING: CONTEMPORARY WRITERS,*
EDITED BY JOSPEH B. ATKINS.

Authors include:

Ace Atkins	Maurice Carlos Ruffin
Steven Barthelme	Margaret Skinner
Jere Hoar	Julie Smith
Corey Mesler	James L. Dickerson
William Boyle	Sheree Renee Thomas
Joseph B. Atkins	Larry Brown

First published in 2005, the *Mojo Triangle* by James L. Dickerson is the first book to define the geographical origins of America's original music—blues, country, jazz, and rock 'n' roll—and link it to America's most powerful and innovative literary tradition. It may be the only book you will ever read that quotes William Faulkner alongside music legends such as B.B. King and Elvis Presley.

Mojo Triangle Travel Guide by Mardi Allen is essential reading if you ever take a road trip into the mystical Triangle—Mississippi, Memphis, Nashville, Muscle Shoals, and New Orleans. The book is filled with interviews, biographical sketches and recommendations for where to find uniquely Southern cuisine, places to find lodging, and listings of music venues where you can listen to blues, jazz, country, and rock 'n' roll.

Mojo Rising: Masters of the Art

CPSIA information can be obtained
at www.ICGtesting.com
Printed in the USA
LVOW10*0149150817

545050LV00001B/1/P